The Accident Victim
&
Other Stories

Gopal Ramanan

This is a work of fiction. Names, characters, businesses, places, events, locales, and incidents are either the products of the author's imagination or used in a fictitious manner. Any resemblance to actual persons, living or dead, or actual events, or other works of fiction, is purely coincidental.

Published by Amazon Publishing Services

1st Edition: December 2020

2nd Edition: August 2021

ISBN: 978-1-5136-7584-8

Other books by the same author:

Radha's Revenge & Other Stories

Murder of a Judge

Strange Happenings at Landings Castle
& Other Humorous Stories

Praise for the author's writing:

This book is dedicated to the memory of my beloved wife

Vidya,

who left our earthly abode far too soon.

"Vidya dearest, you will always be in my heart and soul"

Author's Introduction

In May 2017, my life as I knew it changed forever. That was when my beloved wife Vidya passed away, after a two-year battle with Amyotrophic Lateral Sclerosis, typically known as ALS . Vidya and I had been happily married for 38 years. Words are insufficient to describe how much I miss her. Vidya was the love of my life and my shining star. Her demise has left a huge void in my life, and there is a sadness deep in my heart that never really goes away.

Ever since I was young, I have wanted to write fiction. So, a few months after my beloved wife passed away, I made a huge effort to pull myself together and started to write stories. The positive reviews I received from readers and literary sites to my initial publications encouraged me to keep writing.

This collection of stories was first published in January 2021. Subsequently, I revised and tweaked some of the stories (with some major changes to the title story *The Accident Victim*) and issued the collection as a 2nd edition in August 2021.

G. Ramanan
August 2021

Contents

The Accident Victim

It all happened in one horrific moment.

It was early on a cool morning and the shadows and mist along the roadside were slowly being dissolved by the shimmering rays of early sunlight making its way through gaps in the buildings and trees that lined each side of the road. Traffic was light, and Rajesh leaned back comfortably in his seat as he drove along at a steady pace, enjoying the sights and sounds of of the city coming to life. He saw the traffic signal at the pedestrian crosswalk up ahead turn from green to orange, and took his foot off the accelerator and had gently braked his car to a stop in front of the crosswalk by the time the signal turned red.

But the car on his left, a white BMW traveling in the lane between his car and the sidewalk, accelerated sharply when the traffic signal turned orange. The car's unseen driver was clearly intent on beating the red light. And although the speeding car lost the battle and the traffic signal turned red before the car arrived at the crosswalk, by then it was going so fast that it couldn't have stopped even if the driver wanted to.

Rajesh had glanced to his left when the BMW had sped up, indignation mounting within him. Reckless idiot! These were the kind of people who caused the majority of accidents. Then the expression on his face turned to one of horror when he noticed that a small, slim young lady had stepped off the sidewalk and on to the pedestrian crossing, right into the path of the speeding car. Seeing the traffic signal turn red, she must have thought that it was now safe to cross.

The left edge of the swiftly moving BMW hit the young lady with tremendous force, flinging the girl back on to the concrete sidewalk, where she landed with a sickening thud. The BMW kept going, without slowing down for even an instant, and was soon lost in the traffic up ahead.

For a few moments Rajesh sat frozen, shocked into horrified immobility, his hands clutching the steering wheel, and staring aghast at the spot where the young lady lay sprawled on the sidewalk, motionless. Then movement returned to his frozen limbs, and after checking to see that the lane to his left was clear, he steered his small Fiat quickly over to the sidewalk, sprang out and ran towards the body.

People were already beginning to gather around. Rajesh called out: "Stand back, please! I'm a doctor − let me examine her!"

He knelt down beside the body of the girl. She was lying on her back, unconscious, with blood seeping slowly from the back of her head and pooling on the concrete sidewalk. He felt for her pulse. Her pulse rate was rapid, which Rajesh knew can happen following a traumatic event, as the nervous system pumped adrenaline to cope with the shock. Thank God, she was still alive! Relief surged through him. When he had seen the way she had been flung on to the sidewalk, he had feared the worst.

"Is she dead, *sahib*?" anxiously inquired one of the small group of people who had clustered around.

"She's still alive," Rajesh replied, tersely. He fumbled in his pocket, pulled out his mobile phone, and quickly punched in the three-digit number to call an ambulance. Having done this, he continued his professional examination of the young lady, gently feeling her arms and legs for evidence of broken bones. He didn't attempt to move her; that would be too risky.

"Poor thing — to be hit like that!" another bystander remarked. "It's terrible, the way some of these fancy foreign cars are driven!"

"Must have been one of those young rich kids," said a serious looking elderly gentleman wearing glasses. "They are totally reckless and they think that they can get away with anything."

"Did anyone happen to notice the car's license plate number?" Rajesh asked.

The bystanders shook their heads. "No, it was going too fast," one of them said.

Some twenty minutes later, the ambulance arrived. Rajesh informed the ambulance crew that he was a doctor and quickly explained what had happened. He supervised the ambulance men, making sure that they were very careful as they lifted the inert body of the young lady on to a stretcher and loaded her into the vehicle. He told the ambulance driver to take her to the nearby All India Institute of Medical Sciences Hospital. Rajesh worked there as a Resident Doctor; he had actually been on his way to the hospital, to begin his shift for that day, when he had witnessed the accident.

As soon as the ambulance set off, Rajesh got into his car and headed for the hospital. He felt shaken and had difficulty coming to terms with what had just happened.

Although he had from time to time come upon the scene of a vehicle accident — one could not expect to live in a large city like New Delhi without doing so — he had never before witnessed a hit and run happen right in front of him like this. He took a few deep breaths and tried to calm himself down. His thoughts kept going back to the young lady who had been hit — the poor girl had looked so fragile and helpless as she lay there like a broken doll on the sidewalk.

Arriving at the hospital, he parked in one of the spaces allotted for doctors on duty, and almost ran to the Accident & Emergency Department, located on the ground floor of the AB Wing.

"Tara!" he called out, spotting a nurse he knew by sight. "An unconscious young lady who was brought in by ambulance just a little while ago, where is she?"

"Oh, hello, Dr. Rajesh," Nurse Tara said. "I can take you to where she is being treated."

She led Rajesh through the busy Casualty area to a hospital bed in one corner. The young lady was still unconscious and hooked up to an IV. Rajesh was glad to see that the Senior Resident on call that day was tall, intelligent Dr. Kamakshi Krishnan, who was generally considered to be one of the best doctors in the hospital. Moreover, one of his uncles had known her for over twenty years and she was like an older sister to him.

"How is she?" Rajesh asked.

"She's not in too bad a shape," Dr. Kamakshi said. "She has some bad bruises on her back and arms, but no broken bones. But that wound on her head looks nasty. I've asked for a CAT-scan to ensure that there is no internal bleeding or concussion. What happened to her, do you know?"

Rajesh gave her a quick summary of the accident.

"A hit and run, was it?" Dr. Kamakshi shook her head. "That's too bad. It's a good thing that you were right there, on the spot." She gave Rajesh an encouraging pat on his arm, and added: "She'll be all right, young man. Now, sorry to dash off, but I better attend to some of the other people here."

Rajesh left to make his scheduled rounds. His mind, though, kept straying back to the young lady. She appeared to be some eighteen to twenty years of age. He felt increasing anger towards the unknown driver of the car that had hit her. Hitting a pedestrian as a result of speeding recklessly was bad enough, but to drive off without taking any responsibility! But unfortunately, it happened far too often. He recalled how his cousin's daughter had been sideswiped in similar fashion as she had been walking along the side of a road in Goa, where she had been vacationing at the time. The vehicle that had hit her had driven on without stopping, just like in this instance. His cousin's daughter had been thrown to the ground by the force of the impact; but fortunately for her, aside from a broken nose and some bruises, she had not been badly hurt. Initially, the scar that remained after surgery to reset the broken nose had given rise to a great deal of concern to the girl and her mother; but a renown plastic surgeon in Mumbai, where she lived, had been able to successfully perform cosmetic surgery so that no evidence of that nasty accident remained.

In the afternoon, taking advantage of a brief lull in his busy schedule, Rajesh went over to check on the young lady. He eventually located her in the Emergency Ward. Her eyes were closed and she appeared to be fast asleep, a white gauze bandage wrapped around her head. There was a nurse by the side of her bed, adjusting her IV.

"How is she doing?" he asked.

"Her heart rate and BP are normal," the nurse replied. "She's in considerable pain, though, from the wound on her head and other bruises. We gave her painkillers and sedatives so that she could rest. She's fast asleep now, which is the best thing for her."

"Do you know if the CAT-scan showed any internal injuries?"

The nurse consulted the chart.

"No internal injuries and there appears to be no evidence of concussion," she said.

Rajesh felt a surge of relief.

As he was leaving the hospital that evening after the completion of his shift, he heard a voice call out: "Dr. Rajesh, sir! One moment, please!" He turned to see one of the hospital clerks running towards him.

The clerk drew up, puffing, slightly out of breath. He was a short, tubby young man.

"Sorry to disturb you on your way out," he said, apologetically. "But it's about that young girl who was brought into ER this morning."

"What about her?"

"I heard that you had been checking up on her, sir. I thought that perhaps you know who she is."

Rajesh shook his head. "Unfortunately, I don't. I was a witness to her accident — it happened right in front of me as I was driving to work this morning — and I did a preliminary examination on her at the accident site, but I had never seen her before."

"Oh! I see," the clerk said. "You see, the reason why I asked if you know her is because the girl had absolutely no identification on her — no purse, no handbag, nothing."

Rajesh threw his mind back to the moments prior to the accident, when he had first noticed the girl just as she was about to step into the path of the speeding car. Had she been wearing a handbag or purse slung over one shoulder, the way young ladies typically did? He couldn't be sure. But he was fairly certain that when he had attended to her as she lay on the sidewalk, there had been no handbag or purse on her person or near her body. Perhaps it had been flung off her shoulder when she had been struck, and some bystander had retrieved it. But in that case, the bystander would have handed it over to the ambulance crew, saying that it belonged to the young lady, and Rajesh had not noticed anyone hand over a purse or shoulder bag. Perhaps someone had spotted it lying on the road after the ambulance had left, and turned it over to the police.

He mentioned this to the young clerk, who shook his head doubtfully.

"More likely, sir, is that someone absconded with her purse," the clerk said pessimistically. "Hardly anyone is honest these days. But I'll call the police and check, anyway."

§

The next morning, Rajesh arrived at the hospital half an hour before his shift was scheduled to begin, and made his way to the Emergency Ward. He found the young lady sitting up in bed, a bandage wrapped around her head, still looking weak. She was sipping from a cup of steaming *chai* while one of the nurses, a middle-aged kindly lady with streaks of gray in her hair, hovered around.

The nurse turned to him, smiled and said, "Good morning, Dr. Rajesh. Come to check on your patient?" She turned back to the girl. "This is the doctor who witnessed your accident and attended to you right there."

"Oh, I can't thank you enough!" the young lady said. "You probably saved my life."

She's really very pretty, thought Rajesh. He felt suddenly shy, and said, awkwardly, "I was just doing my job, Miss ___" He left the sentence unfinished and looked inquiringly at her.

The girl's face clouded over and her eyes pooled with tears. "Oh, I wish I could remember my name! But I can't recall anything – not a thing!" She began to sob abjectly, with her face screwed up like that of a child's, and the hand holding the teacup began to shake. Some of the tea sloshed over the sides of the cup and formed large brown spots on the white sheet covering her from the waist down.

"There, there, dear," the nurse said, deftly taking the teacup from her shaking hand and placing it on the breakfast tray. She handed the girl a tissue from a box nearby. "Don't you worry, it will all come back to you soon, I'm sure. Now, you just lie back and take some rest." The nurse gently coaxed the young lady into lying back on her pillow. After making sure that she had stopped crying and was lying down comfortably, the nurse glanced at Rajesh, and with a tilt of her head, indicated that he should follow her out of the room.

Out in the corridor, the nurse said: "Poor thing! Her memory's totally gone."

"Can't she remember anything?" asked Rajesh.

The nurse shook her head. "Not a thing. She has no idea who she is, where she lived, who her parents are, whether she has any relatives — nothing! Tell me, what happened to her, exactly? Her file mentions that she was involved in an accident, but doesn't provide any details."

Rajesh filled her in on what had happened.

"She's lucky to be alive," the nurse said. "When she was flung back and hit her head on the sidewalk, it must have wiped out her memory. That happens sometimes, as you know." Then she added, optimistically, "Perhaps, after a few days of rest, her memory will return."

Rajesh got into the habit of checking in on the girl whenever time permitted. After three days, she was considered well enough to be transferred to the general ward. On most days, after his shift was over, or before his shift began, he made his way to the young lady's bedside and chatted with her, attempting to get her to recall some detail, however trivial, of her past life. He described the location of her accident in detail, hoping that it would stir up some dormant memory as to why she had been at that particular spot that morning. Over the course of a week, he talked to her about family life, hoping that it might enable her to recall if she had parents or siblings or other relatives in town or elsewhere; he talked to her about current and past events in the world outside the hospital; he even talked to her about movies, TV shows, books, and sports, in the hope that it might trigger some recollection of her past interests and in turn lead her mind gradually

9

to a remembrance of who she was. But none of his valiant efforts bore fruit; memories of her past life remained stubbornly blank. She wept often in frustration and fear.

Surprisingly, she was able to recall in detail everything that had happened from the time she had regained consciousness in the hospital. Rajesh from time to time tested her current memory by asking her to recall what he had said to her the prior day or the day before that, and what the nurse had said, and what she had eaten, and she was able to do so without a problem. Their regular conversations revealed her to be intelligent and apparently well educated.

His frequent visits to the young lady's bedside had not gone unnoticed by the hospital staff, and Rajesh found himself having to endure quite a bit of teasing from his colleagues. His attempts to explain that he was only trying to help the girl regain her memory were met with grins, leers, and winks, often accompanied by a prod in the ribs or a hearty slap on his back. Rajesh eventually gave up trying to defend his actions. He only hoped that the ribald comments about the two of them wouldn't get to the young lady's ears; she was dealing with enough as it was.

Since the girl had no clothes of her own, aside from what she had been wearing at the time of the accident, Rajesh brought her some of his mother's cotton *sarees* to wear. Rajesh's middle-aged mother lived with him and he had told his mother all about the accident and his mother had been only too glad to help out.

After ten days, when the young lady was still unable to recall anything of her life prior to the accident, Rajesh asked Dr. Chitra Chari, who was a neurologist and also a good friend, to examine her.

After completing a thorough examination, Dr. Chitra took Rajesh aside and said: "She appears to have what is termed Retrograde Amnesia. This is marked by the inability to recall past information prior to a traumatic event, such as the accident in her case. While cases of such amnesia are rare, they have been known to happen, and can be caused by a sharp blow to the head. However, what is interesting in such cases is that the patient will retain normal ability to form new memories after the traumatic event. That too appears to be true in her case; as you yourself have noticed, she's able to remember pretty much everything that has happened after regaining consciousness in the hospital."

"When will she able to regain her prior memories?" asked Rajesh.

"It's hard to say," Dr. Chitra replied. "Case studies indicate that while some patients recover quickly, in a matter of weeks or months, in others, it has taken years for the prior memories to return. In many cases, there is a spontaneous recovery, in which the old memories suddenly come flooding back. The good news is that people with Retrograde Amnesia are able to function quite normally; it does not affect their intelligence, and usually, their personality remains intact. In her case, there does not seem to be any other ecological or psychometric evidence of cognitive impairment. In fact, her intelligence appears to be above average, and she appears to be well educated."

"Yes, I had noticed that," Rajesh said. "Well, let's hope for the best. Thanks much for examining her, Chitra."

"Glad to do it. Call me if you need any further help."

§

A few days later, when Rajesh was in the hospital canteen, having a quick lunch, one of the Hospital Administrators approached him and said, "Dr. Rajesh, the physicians who have been attending to that young lady who's lost her memory feel that she is well enough to be discharged. We can't keep her in the hospital indefinitely, since we need the bed for other patients. I've been told that her memories of her past still haven't returned, and she still doesn't know who she is?"

"Yes, that's correct," Rajesh said.

"In a case like this," the Administrator continued, "Where a person has lost his or her memory and has no money, nothing, we make arrangements to have that person placed in a shelter or orphanage or some such place after being discharged from the hospital."

"I'm aware of that, sir," Rajesh said.

"Very good! I heard that you have been seeing quite a bit of her, which is why I sought you out to let you know..."

Rajesh flushed. "I've just been trying to do what I can to help her regain her memory. I don't know if you've been told, sir, that I was a witness to the accident that wiped out her memory."

The Administrator looked startled. "No, I didn't know that. Well, that certainly puts things in a different light: naturally you would take a personal interest in such a patient." He got up and said, "Anyway, let me begin the process to get the young lady transferred to a shelter."

When driving home that evening, Rajesh thought about what the Hospital Administrator had told him. The realization that the young lady — who obviously was intelligent, cultured, and well educated – was going to be sent to a women's shelter or orphanage to live there until her memory returned made him feel depressed. He was aware that while those places tried to do their best, they tended to be overcrowded and they catered more to young runaways and abused women and children from the poorer sections of society. And sadly, there had been reports of sexual abuse at some of the shelters.

Then he was struck by a sudden idea. Why not have the girl live with him and his mother until her memory returned? The more he examined his idea, the more he liked it.

He could easily accommodate her in his comfortable three-bedroom flat, left to him by his father, who had passed away some five years ago. Even with him and his mother occupying two of the bedrooms, there was still the third one available. He was currently utilizing the 3rd bedroom as his study, but very little adjustments needed to be made to convert it back to a regular bedroom. There was already a large futon in there that folded out into a bed, and the room also contained a cupboard that was mostly empty, where the young lady could keep her clothes. He could easily move the computer he had in there to his own bedroom. And the young lady could use the guest bathroom located in the corridor; he and his mother each had their own separate bathrooms, attached to each of their bedrooms.

Then he thought, *I really should discuss this with my mother first, before suddenly springing a guest on her for an indefinite stay.*

As soon as he got home, he talked to his mother about his plan as he sat at the dining table, drinking his evening *chai*.

At first, his mother sounded doubtful. "It's a big responsibility, *beta*," she said. "The girl is young, of a marriageable age. Our neighbors will surely gossip – you know how some of them are! They will say to each other, 'Who is that young lady who has suddenly shown up at Rajesh's house?' They will come around on some pretext or the other and probe and pry and try to find out who she is."

"But, mother, does it matter? Let the neighbors think whatever they want!"

"I don't want us to be the focus of gossip," his mother demurred. "And another thing: I haven't even met this young lady. I don't know what she's like. What if the two of us can't get along?"

This aspect had not occurred to Rajesh. He said reassuringly, "Mother, I have been seeing her and talking to her daily for a week, and I can tell you this much: she appears to be intelligent, cultured, well educated, and most important of all, she also appears to be a very sweet person."

"That does sound better," his mother admitted. "But still, having a total stranger around –"

"Well, look at it this way," Rajesh said. "What if one of your close friends suddenly called you and said: 'My daughter is coming to Delhi to look for a job, so could you accommodate her for a few weeks till she finds one and gets her own place?' You wouldn't say no, would you, even if you had never met the girl? Actually, come to think of it, didn't that happen to one of your brothers, when he accommodated a friend's daughter in his house for a whole summer?"

"That's true," admitted his mother. "Very well, you can bring the young lady and have her stay here until her memory returns. I must say, you are being extraordinarily kind to her."

"You're the one who raised me to be kind, mother," Rajesh retorted.

"That's right — blame it on me," his mother said, but since she was smiling, Rajesh knew that she was pleased by the compliment, and, he thought, she was in all likelihood also pleased that he *was* being kind. "I remember when you were a young boy, you would bring home every stray kitten or puppy you found wandering around. It used to drive your poor father wild."

She went on: "Now, let's return to the problem of having to deal with what our neighbors will say when you bring this young lady home. Your mention of my brother gave me an idea — why don't I tell any one who asks that she is my niece, my brother's daughter? I could say that she has just completed her degree and wanted to come to Delhi to look for a job. It's only natural that I would have no objections to having my own niece live here with us while she looks for a job."

"That's a good idea," Rajesh said, relieved. He began to get up from the table.

But his mother said: "Wait! Don't go yet — I just thought of something. This girl's memory is completely gone, correct? She cannot remember anything of her past life?"

"Yes, that's right."

"Then what if some of our nosey neighbors talk to her

15

directly? They are likely to ask her, 'Oh, what was your degree in? Perhaps we could help you land a job. We know Mr. So-and-so, a very influential man, and he will certainly be able to find you a good job.' You know how eager they always are to show off their connections! Then the girl might blurt out that she can't remember anything of her past life, can't remember if she has a degree, even. What are we to say then?"

Rajesh sat down again and complained, "Mother, this is getting hopelessly complicated! All I want to do is help this poor girl!"

"I know, *beta*," his mother said. "But one has to think of these things beforehand — I don't want to come up with an awkward explanation on the spot, after the girl arrives." She pondered for a bit, then said: "How about this: instead of saying that she has come to Delhi looking for a job, why don't we tell those who ask that she had been in a bad accident in the small town where she lived with her parents, and as a result of the accident, lost her memory. Then her father — my brother — brought her here to New Delhi because better treatments are available here, and also because you are a doctor. We could further say that my brother had to go back immediately because he had to attend to the businesses he owns in his town, and so he left her in our care. That would make sense to our nosey neighbors, I think. Also, the advantage of this story is that the part about her being in an accident and losing her memory is true, so it would fit in with anything the girl might blurt out about not being able to recollect her past."

"All right, mother, whatever you think is best," Rajesh said, sighing. "I still think all this obfuscation is unnecessary. Let our nosey neighbors think what they

16

want!"

"You won't have to put up with all their prying and questioning – you'll be off at work!" his mother retorted. "So, anyway, that's settled. Now, let us decide on what we're going to name this young lady."

Rajesh looked puzzled. "What do you mean?"

"Well, we can't just say, 'Hey, you!' whenever we want to address her, can we?" his mother asked, looking at him with considerable amusement. "Besides, our neighbors will want to know her name, so let's think of one."

Rajesh buried his head in his hands and said, "Mother, if I hear about our neighbors once more, my head's going to explode! You pick a name. I'm not good at that sort of thing."

"Let me think of a good name," his mother said, getting up. "I have to go and finish making dinner. I'll think about it while cooking."

"And I am going to go for a walk – I really need one!" announced Rajesh. "I never thought that so many societal conventions would be involved in trying to help someone!"

"That's because you men never think of such things!" his mother retorted, rising and heading to the kitchen. "You just barge ahead, willy-nilly, with no regard for what others may think."

As he walked around in nearby Gulmohar Park, Rajesh thought about his mother's parting shot about barging ahead without regards to what others may think. He began to be assailed by self-doubt. Was he doing just that? He was blindly assuming that the young lady wouldn't mind coming to live with him and his mother until her memory returned. What if she didn't want to? Perhaps she might prefer to go to a shelter or orphanage. That aspect had not occurred to him before. Why was this getting so complicated? He took a deep breath, and forced himself to calm down.

I'll talk to her as soon as I can tomorrow, and place the two options before her, and let her decide, he thought.

Later that evening, when they were having their dinner together, Rajesh's mother remarked, "I've come up with a name for the girl."

Rajesh looked at her expectantly.

"We'll call her Geetha," his mother said. "In honor of my older sister's daughter, who passed away due to cancer at quite a young age."

§

The next morning, the practical complexities of his proposed plan of action began to dawn on Rajesh. Would the hospital allow him to take the young lady to his home? He thought not. He could envision the Administrator becoming upset and saying: "Dr. Rajesh, what you are proposing is a serious breach of our normal procedure. I cannot condone it. I could get into serious trouble."

So, what to do?

Perhaps he ought to talk to his close friend and colleague Dr. K.G. Srinivas. K.G., as he was called by his friends, was a boisterous fellow who loved bending and breaking rules just for the fun of it. He and K.G. had gone through high school, pre-med and medical school together, and had become close friends in spite of their stark differences in temperament: Rajesh was the quiet, serious type while K.G. was fun-loving and mischievous. He was also very intelligent. Rajesh felt that K.G. would be able to come up with some good ideas for circumventing the rules so that Rajesh could take the young lady to his flat rather than have her go to a shelter. And what was most important was that despite his fun-loving nature, K.G. was a kind-hearted chap who could be relied upon to keep the matter secret if told to do so by an old friend like Rajesh.

Accordingly, when he had the chance, Rajesh dragged K.G. off to a quiet corner of the hospital canteen and poured out the story of the young lady and his proposed plan. "The young lady is intelligent, and appears to be well educated and cultured. I just can't see someone like that being placed in a shelter. As you know, they are mostly full of runaways or victims of domestic abuse and so on."

"My serious friend Rajesh, actually planning to do something so daring — taking a strange girl into your home!" K.G. exclaimed, looking delighted. "I never thought that I'd see the day! This sounds like the story-line of one of those Bollywood movies. You must have fallen hard for the pretty young damsel." His eyes twinkling, he began to sing the opening lines of a popular love song.

"Stop ragging, will you," pleaded Rajesh. "Can you come up with a way for me to get around the hospital rules and take the girl to my place?"

"Let me think for a minute." K.G. became serious and leaned back in his chair and stared into space. Rajesh watched him anxiously.

Finally K.G. turned to him and said, "Rajesh, here's what you can do. Let the hospital go ahead and complete the paperwork for placing the young lady in a suitable shelter. I'll find out which one has agreed to take her. Don't worry, I have my ways for finding out such things. I'll let you know which shelter she's being sent to. After she has been sent there, you go over and take her to your flat."

"But what will I tell the people who run the shelter, so that they allow me to take her from there?" asked Rajesh. "I'm sure they won't just allow just anyone to come barging in and her take away; they would feel a responsibility towards a person who's been placed under their care."

"Come, come, there's any of a half-dozen things you could tell them," K.G. said. "Here's something you could say that will sound convincing. Tell them that you're the doctor who's been treating her in the hospital — which is true — and so you know that she has lost her memory. Tell them that you and your mother are in need of a live-in maid, and you would like to employ this young lady in that capacity, so as to help her out —"

Noticing the indignant look on Rajesh's face, K.G. sighed in exasperation and said, "Of course you're not going to actually employ the young lady as your maid, silly! You're just going to say that to those who run the shelter to provide a plausible reason to take her into your home."

"Oh, right," Rajesh said.

"I just thought of something else —— what might really help is to convince your mother to accompany you to the shelter. The shelter's administrators will probably be more easily convinced to release the young lady into your custody if they are able to actually see your kindly-looking middle-aged mother. Your mother can chip in and confirm that she does, indeed, live with you. That way, the shelter's administrators won't have doubts that they might be releasing the young lady to a single man who might have evil intentions, and have qualms about the whole thing." K.G. paused, grinned and said, "Let's face it, Rajesh, you look like the archetype Bollywood villain."

"Ha! You're must be thinking of yourself," retorted Rajesh. He passed a hand over his forehead. "Gosh, I hope I can say all this convincingly."

"Oh, my God!" K.G. said. "You're hopeless. Tell you what I'll do — I'll meet you at the shelter. Let me do all the talking, and I guarantee that you'll leave with your little *mehbooba* in tow."

"Stop calling her that!" Rajesh said.

Rajesh made his way through the hospital to the young lady's bedside. After the usual greetings were exchanged, he said to her: "It appears that you're now considered well enough to be discharged from the hospital."

A look of alarm came over her face, and her voice trembled. "But, where will I go?"

Rajesh said, gently, "Since you are still unable to recall anything about yourself, what normally happens is that arrangements are made to have you placed in one of the women's shelters or orphanages in town."

The young lady looked worried but bravely said, "Well, if that's the process, I guess I have no choice."

Rajesh looked around. None of the nurses or other

doctors were nearby. He sat down on a stool next to the bed, lowered his voice and said, "I've thought of a way to help you avoid living at a shelter or orphanage, and stay at a nicer place. But please keep your voice low, I don't want anyone else to hear."

She looked at him anxiously and nodded.

"You can stay with me and my mother, until your memory returns. As you know, my mother lives with me." During the course of their daily conversations, he had told her quite a bit about himself. "So it won't be as though you would be moving in with just me. I have discussed this plan with my mother, and I can assure you that she will take good care of you. I have a three-bedroom flat, and you will have your own bedroom. And," he added, mustering up a smile, "My mother will ensure that I behave well."

The girl tried to muster up a smile in return, then her look of anxiety returned. She looked down at her clasped hands and said hesitantly, "You are being really kind, but could I have some time to think it over?"

"Why, certainly," Rajesh said, inwardly cursing himself for not having made the suggestion. *What is wrong with me? How could have I expected her to make such a monumental decision on the spot?*

He said, gently, "I'll go and take care of my rounds and return in a couple of hours. You can tell me then."

When he returned, the young lady was looking a great deal more cheerful. She smiled at him and said softly, "I think I would like to stay with you and your mother instead of living at a shelter."

He returned her smile, and said, "Very good. Now, here's the plan…"

§

On the evening of the day the young lady was discharged from the hospital and sent to the shelter, Rajesh drove there after work, with his mother accompanying him. K.G. had been as good as his word and had found out which shelter the young lady had been sent to. He said that he would meet them there, so that he could later drive back home in his own car.

Rajesh had talked to his mother of the scheme K.G. had come up with, and how important it was for her to accompany him. His mother had been reluctant at first, but he had managed to convince her eventually. Now, driving to the shelter, he was feeling worried. *I hope my mother carries out her part properly.*

K.G. met them in the parking lot of the shelter, and they went inside together. K.G. explained to the shelter's administrators that Rajesh was the doctor who had been treating the young lady who had totally lost her memory and who had just been transferred to the shelter from AIIMS Hospital. He explained how Rajesh and his mother, being in need of a live-in maid, had decided that they would like to hire the young lady, as a way of helping her. He told the administrators that if the girl's memory returned while she in their employ, Rajesh would ensure that she was taken back home and reunited with her parents or relatives or whoever she had been living with before the tragic accident had wiped out her memory. As a clincher, K.G. pointed out that since Rajesh was a doctor who was very familiar with the young lady's case, his home was the best place for the girl. K.G.'s narrative was very convincing.

The shelter's administrators were quickly convinced and only too glad to release the young lady into Rajesh's custody. The shelter was overcrowded with more homeless youngsters and adults to take care of than they could handle, and the administrators congratulated themselves on the fact that the young lady had been fortunate to find a good home so quickly. It would look good on their reports.

Naturally, there was a good deal of paperwork to be filled out, and Rajesh had to sign quite a few documents. All this took some time. Meanwhile, the young lady was brought into the waiting room. Rajesh's mother led her to a quiet corner and talked to her earnestly.

Eventually, all the paperwork was completed and they were able to leave. By then, it was late evening. Rajesh's mother held the girl's hand as they walked towards where Rajesh's car was parked. The young lady looked happy but subdued.

Rajesh hung back and shook his friend's hand warmly. "I can't thank you enough, K.G., for your help today."

"Think nothing of it, *yaar*," K.G. said. He clapped Rajesh on the back and with a devilish grin, lowered his voice and added: "Just make sure that you send me a wedding invitation!" With that parting shot, he dashed off.

"Would you prefer to sit in the front passenger seat or in the back with my mother?" Rajesh asked the young lady after unlocking the car doors.

Seeing her hesitate, Rajesh's mother quickly said: "Please sit in front, *beti*. You will have a much better view of everything as we drive back home, which will be nice for you after all these days in the hospital. I am quite used to sitting alone in the back."

As they drove off, Rajesh said: "By the way, since you can't remember your name, my mother decided that we will call you Geetha, till your memory returns." In an attempt to lighten the situation, which he hoped she wouldn't take offense to, he smiled and added, "It's better than calling you Miss X."

"Being called Geetha is infinitely better than Miss X," the girl replied, smiling faintly.

Rajesh drove slowly, so as not to alarm Geetha. From time to time, he stole a quick glance at her out of the corners of his eyes. She was looking around at the buildings and shops they were passing by with interest. After a while, she said despondently, "I wish I could remember something — anything! None of these areas seem familiar."

"Your memory will return soon, I'm sure," said Rajesh, soothingly. Then, partly to distract her and partly so that she could become familiar with the surroundings, he began to talk about the various neighborhoods they were passing through. "This area is called Gautam Nagar. We're headed for the Hauz Khas Apartments, which is where I live. I am fortunate in that my father bought this flat a long time ago, when it was much more affordable. When he passed away five years ago, it came to me. I certainly couldn't afford to buy a flat there now — prices have shot up like anything! The best thing is, it's close to AIIMS, where I got my medical degree and where I'm working now, as you know."

Rajesh was normally a quiet person, but now he

forced himself to keep chattering away to take Geetha's mind off her present situation. *It must be so scary for her, not knowing who she is, or anything of her past, and going off to live with strangers,* he thought. *Even though she's become somewhat familiar with me during her hospital stay, it's not like she's known me for a while. And she met my mother for the first time today.* He felt overwhelmed with sympathy for her plight but didn't know what to say to reassure her in addition to what he had already said to her in the hospital, so kept up his chatter about the areas they were passing through, with his mother contributing an occasional comment from the rear seat.

As soon as they entered the flat, Rajesh's mother turned to Geetha and said: "My dear, please think of this as your own home, and think of me as your mother. Don't hesitate to ask for anything."

The kind words brought tears to Geetha's eyes. "You are both being so kind! I cannot thank you enough." Rajesh's mother held her hand tight and after the girl's sobs subsided, said gently, "Come, let me show you to your bedroom. You can have a quick wash up if you want to while I set out our dinner."

During the meal, Geetha ate silently, her head lowered. Rajesh and his mother kept up an animated chatter about everything from the latest movies to politics, trying to make the atmosphere as cheerful as possible.

After dinner was over, Geetha, on her own, helped Rajesh's mother clear the table and take the remaining food back into the kitchen and helped her to wash up the dinner plates and vessels. After this was done, she said that she would like to go and lie down in her room. Rajesh's mother accompanied her there, saying that she wanted to ensure that she had everything she needed.

Rajesh, sitting in his armchair in the living room and watching TV, could hear them talking, but couldn't make out what was being said.

After a while, his mother came out of Geetha's bedroom, closing the door behind her. She came over and sat down on the sofa and sighed. Rajesh looked at her, questioningly.

"She's gone to sleep, poor thing," his mother said. "It's the best thing for her right now."

His mother sighed again, her face filled with sadness. "I just can't imagine how hard it must be for her — not knowing your own name, where you came from, who your parents are — nothing! It must be so very scary. You know, we all take our memories for granted, but our memories are an integral part of us, and they play a large role in making us who we are."

"Yes, it must be really hard for her," Rajesh said, feelingly. "Let us hope that her memories return soon." He recounted to his mother what Dr. Chitra had told him after examining the young lady.

His mother listened intently, then said: "I will take her to our local temple tomorrow. Perhaps the priest knows of special prayers we can perform for a case like this. In any case, going to the temple will surely bring her more peace of mind."

The next morning, when Rajesh came to the kitchen to ask his mother for his morning tea — his mother was an early riser, and usually got up well before he did — he was pleasantly surprised to see Geetha there, helping his mother make breakfast. She looked rested and more happier than the prior evening, and said "Good morning" to him, shyly.

"Looks like Geetha is an early riser, like me," his mother remarked, smiling.

"I think it's because I went to bed so early last night," Geetha said.

"Rajesh, why don't you go and sit at the dining table, and we'll bring you your tea," his mother said.

Rajesh obediently went and sat at the dining table, and unfolded the morning newspaper, which he had picked up from outside the front door of his flat.

Somewhat to his surprise, it was Geetha who brought him his tea. She placed it in front of him, and waited while he took a sip.

"It's delicious," he said, smiling at her. "Thank you."

She blushed when he said that and looked happy, and retreated back into the kitchen.

Later, the three of them had breakfast together. Geetha was more animated this morning, and joined in the conversation.

All day long at work, Rajesh's thoughts kept drifting back to the young lady. He had been greatly cheered by what he had seen in the morning — his mother and Geetha appeared to be getting along well. He hoped it would last.

By the end of one week, all his trepidations about bringing her to his home had vanished. Geetha had settled in amazingly well. It seemed like the most natural thing in the world to see her moving around the flat and helping his mother in the kitchen, and sit with them at the dining table and in the living room, joining in the conversation. Rajesh was glad that his mother now had company during the day. They discovered that Geetha was quite a good cook — Rajesh recalled that Dr. Chitra had said to him that amnesia victims usually retained their natural skills intact, citing the case of a teenage boy who had total amnesia but could play the violin really well, despite never taking any lessons after losing his memory. Geetha and his mother took to trying out new mouth-watering recipes, and Rajesh complained that they were spoiling him and he was putting on weight.

Whenever he was able to get home at a reasonable hour, Rajesh was accustomed to taking an evening walk in nearby Gulmohar Park when the weather was nice, as it was now. The park contained shady trees, playgrounds, and a few old ruins, and taking a long walk there helped him to shake off the tensions of the day and keep himself fit. He preferred walking outdoors to going to the gym, unless the weather was so bad that it rendered a walk outdoors impractical.

Rajesh's mother encouraged Geetha to go with him on his evening walks, saying: "It's good for you to get some exercise after being cooped up in the flat all day long."

Rajesh and Geetha became quite a familiar sight as they walked together around the park and large grassy playgrounds. During these walks, they both discovered that they had a great deal in common, with similar tastes in music, books, and films. Geetha was delighted with Rajesh's large collection of mystery novels, which he had kept in his study, which was now her bedroom; she remarked that it must have been her favorite genre prior to her memory loss, since she enjoyed reading them so much.

As Rajesh's mother had foretold, the neighbors were full of curiosity about the new arrival to Rajesh's household. But his mother's explanation that Geetha was her brother's daughter, sent by her family to recuperate from a bad accident, seemed to satisfy them. The neighbors were very sympathetic when they learnt that she had lost her memory, and some of the older ladies were full of suggestions for homemade herbal remedies and prayers that would help the poor girl.

A fortnight passed swiftly by. Geetha had become very much a part of the household, and Rajesh truly enjoyed having her around. His mother appeared to be happy having Geetha at home, as well.

But Geetha's memories of her past life stubbornly refused to return. While she appeared to have bravely taken her situation in stride, there were times when Rajesh thought he heard her crying in her bedroom late at night. He had been tempted to go and knock on her door and offer words of comfort, but his innate modesty made him shrink from invading her privacy.

After a few weeks, Geetha began to talk about getting a job. She said she felt bad that she was adding to their household expenses without contributing anything in the way of income. Rajesh assured her that she needn't feel that way and pointed out that she was helping his mother a great deal; but added that if Geetha really did want to take up a job, he wouldn't stand in her way and would help her find one.

§

One night a month later, a little past ten-thirty, Rajesh was sitting in his armchair in the living room, going through a medical journal that he subscribed to, when his mother came in, sat down on the sofa. Geetha had already retired to her bedroom, and they were alone.

His mother whispered, "*Beta*, I want to discuss something important with you, but keep your voice low."

Rajesh looked at her inquiringly.

His mother said, "Geetha is a very nice girl. She's sweet, intelligent, respectful, and helps me so much around the house."

Rajesh smiled. "That's nice, mother."

"But it has been a month and her memories have not returned," his mother said.

"It's still early, mother. Give it time."

"But *beta*, what if, after six months or so, her memory still hasn't come back? Are you going to send her off to a women's shelter then?"

"No, of course not!" Rajesh said, indignantly.

"Then don't you think we need to think about her future?"

Rajesh said nothing. He had a feeling that he knew what his mother was going to say next.

"*Beta*, I've mentioned this to you before — it's time you got married. But you have told me often that you don't like the idea of the traditional 'arranged marriage' where you meet the girl formally once, in the company of her parents, and then the wedding is fixed up. You have said that you prefer to marry someone you know well and not a complete stranger. Well, here's your chance to marry a nice girl whom you've been able to get to know really well. I know you like her very much."

Rajesh could not deny this. It was true, he liked Geetha far more than most of the other girls he had met over the years: she was intelligent, easy to talk to, appeared to be well educated, and most important of all, she appeared to be a mature, sweet person who did not pout and make a fuss about things. He admired her bravery in carrying on as best as she could under the circumstances; many others would have broken down completely.

His mother went on, "And honestly, I couldn't ask for a better daughter-in-law than Geetha."

Rajesh said, "But we know nothing about her."

"What does that matter? I can tell that she is well educated and sophisticated. You've probably come to the same conclusion, too."

"Oh, most definitely!" Rajesh said. "But when I said that we know nothing about her, what I was meant was, we don't know if she's already married, or engaged to someone else."

His mother said, "No, I don't think she's married; she doesn't have a *mangalsutra* around her neck. But it's possible that she had been engaged to someone."

"In that case, how can I ask her to marry me? It wouldn't be right. Also, you talk of me marrying her, but how do you know if she would want to marry *me*? Perhaps she has other ideas about what to do with her life, even if her memories don't return."

"Why wouldn't she want to marry you — you are a very nice, decent young man in an honorable profession," said his mother, with the irrefutable logic that mothers possess. "You are responsible and hard-working and you don't waste your time going to nightclubs and parties and other frivolous pursuits. You should see the number of inquiries I get about you every week from the parents of unmarried daughters!"

Rajesh was startled at hearing this. "You do?"

"But leaving that aside, I believe Geetha likes you very much — I have seen the way she looks at you sometimes."

Rajesh felt himself blushing. Somewhat to his surprise, he found warmth and happiness spreading through him. Forcing himself to come back to reality, he said: "But, mother, there are other things we surely must consider. Even if Geetha doesn't regain the memories of her past, what if later on her family tracks her down here, somehow? To find her married to me, a total stranger to them? Just think of what a huge shock it would be to the family."

His mother stayed silent for a while, then sighed deeply. "You're right, *beta*. It's all such a muddle, isn't it?"

Rajesh said soothingly, "In any case, there's no rush to decide on her future. It's only been about six weeks since she lost her memory. Let's wait and see what happens. I'm willing to let Geetha live here as long as she wants, as long as you are, too."

"Oh, most certainly! I truly enjoy having her around." His mother got up. "Well, it's getting late. I'm off to bed."

"Goodnight, mother."

After she had left, Rajesh continued to sit in the living room, deep in thought. Prior to his mother broaching the subject just now, he had never even thought about about marrying Geetha. But now that his mother had planted the seed in his mind, he found himself thinking that Geetha possessed all the qualities he desired in a lifetime companion. He also had to admit that the sight of her made him feel very happy inside, and he enjoyed being in her company, and he thought about her often while he was at work. He wondered, *is that love? Have I fallen in love with her?*

Working as a doctor in one of the busiest hospitals in town, Rajesh had found little time for romantic liaisons. Moreover, from childhood on, he had been shy around girls and that shyness had not left him once he had grown into a young man. At work, he had to deal with young female nurses and young female doctors, but to him that was different, it was on a professional basis, so he had no problems interacting with them. When he was at work, his mind was so focused on his job that he did not view his female co-workers as anything other than that. Moreover, the majority of the female nurses and doctors he encountered at work were already married. He had really never tried to meet girls outside of work by going to nightclubs or parties; he had never felt comfortable in that kind of environment. The few times he had been dragged to a nightclub or party by enthusiastic friends, he had not liked the kind of girls he had met there. In the rare instances when he had gone to a movie, or to a restaurant, it had been in the company of one or more of his male friends.

His thoughts turned to the vexing problem of discovering who Geetha really was. He had asked his mother and Geetha to get into the habit of scanning the Missing Persons ads in the daily newspaper. He had emphasized to them that any such ad would have been placed by those concerned under her real name, which she herself did not know; so they would have to go through the details on all of them, to see if the description matched Geetha. The Missing Persons ads also included a photograph in most instances. But sadly, they had not spotted any description or photo that resembled Geetha thus far.

Rajesh had discovered that if he wished to check all the Missing Person Reports that had been filed with the Police since the day Geetha had been struck by that car and lost her memory, he would have to go in person to the Police Station. Even though it was the year 1998 and technology had advanced rapidly over the past decade, it was still impossible to access the Police Department's Missing Persons datafile from one's home computer. So, one evening about ten days after the accident, when he had found the time to do so, Rajesh had gone to the nearest police station. He had reasoned that surely Geetha's parents or some other relative (if her parents had already passed away) would have filed a Missing Person Report with the police.

The police station had been terribly crowded, and after waiting for well over an hour, Rajesh had been shown to a young police officer's desk. The officer had asked for the name of the missing person, and an expression of exasperation had come over his face when Rajesh had confessed that he did not know. Rajesh had hurriedly explained the circumstances, stressing that the girl had completely lost her memory. When the Police Officer had heard that young lady was living safely with Rajesh and his mother, it had become clear that this case would not be a priority and had proceeded to lecture Rajesh about the vast number of missing person cases the Delhi Police had to deal with. The Police Officer had said that over 22,000 missing persons were reported each year in the city, the majority of them young children. He had gone on to say that the focus of the Delhi Police was on tracing children under the age of 14, since they were significantly more vulnerable to exploitation by human traffickers. The official had taken down his description of Geetha, and Rajesh's name, address and phone number, and promised to contact him if anything regarding her turned up. Rajesh had not heard from the police since.

Busy as Rajesh was with his job, he had not had the time to follow up with the police regularly. The few times that he had called the police about Geetha, someone at the other end had politely taken down his inquiry, but he had never heard anything back.

Perhaps he should go to the Police Station again, he thought, and ask if they would allow him to review all the Missing Person Reports that had been filed in the past month. He realized that meant having to go over a vast number of such reports, which in turn meant that he would have to set aside a great deal of time — he probably would have to do it on his day off. Perhaps the reports were filed by age group, which would make the task somewhat easier.

A sudden idea struck Rajesh. If he himself didn't have the time, why not ask Geetha to go to the nearest police station, say once a week, and go through the Missing Person Reports that had been filed with the police?

He berated himself for not thinking of this sooner.

If more time went by and Geetha's memory still did not return, perhaps he should employ the services of one of the detective agencies that existed in town — they might be able to track down Geetha's parents or other relatives or someone who knew her well. He could try to find a reputable agency by asking his friends and colleagues. There would no doubt be a steep fee charged by such a service, since they had so little to go on except the site and date of the accident, but Rajesh found himself thinking that he was prepared to pay a steep fee, it came to that; he wished to leave no stone unturned in his quest to help the young lady discover her real identity, knowing that if he was successful, it would mean that she would no longer live with him and his mother. But, so what? It was more important for her to go back to her own people, live in her own home. After all, if she was willing, they could continue to see each other (and based on what his mother had said, she probably would be).

§

The next day, when Geetha accompanied him on his evening walk, Rajesh found himself feeling awkward and tongue-tied; his mother's remarks on the previous night about marrying her, and a reflection of his own feelings about her, made it hard for him to chat easily with her as he usually did. Possibly sensing his mood, Geetha too was mostly silent.

Their route through the Park took them past one of the playgrounds, where a group of young boys were playing cricket. Suddenly, the air was filled with a chorus of boyish shouts: "Uncle! Auntie! Look out!"

Before either Rajesh or Geetha could react, a red, hard cricket ball came whizzing through the air and struck Geetha hard on her temple. She staggered and fell against Rajesh, who lost his balance, and both of them collapsed unceremoniously on to the grassy playground.

Rajesh scrambled to his hands and knees, staring aghast at Geetha's prone figure lying on the grassy field, unconscious. His mind immediately went back to the last time he had seen her lying thus, and he was filled with fear and anguish. He frantically patted her cheeks, calling out desperately: "Geetha! Geetha!"

The boys came running up.

"Uncle! We're so sorry!"

"Is auntie all right?"

Rajesh was fumbling for his mobile phone, getting ready to call for an ambulance, when Geetha suddenly moaned and opened her eyes. Her hand went to her temple, and she said, weakly, "What - what happened? My head hurts!"

"Geetha!" cried Rajesh, with a surge of relief. "Don't try to move! I'm going to call for an ambulance."

His injunction not to move didn't appear to register with her, for she pushed herself up to a sitting position. Her hand went to her temple again, where a large bruise had formed, and she winced. "What happened?" she repeated.

"You were hit by a cricket ball," Rajesh explained. "They're quite hard, you know, and this one came flying at tremendous speed."

Geetha's eyes wandered over him, over the group of young boys clustered around them, and around the park and playground. A puzzled expression came into her eyes.

"Where am I?" she asked.

"Why, we're in Gulmohar Park, which is where we usually take our evening walk," Rajesh replied. "Don't you remember?"

"Evening walk?" Geetha echoed. Her eyes went around the park, and the puzzled expression on her face deepened. "But - but, where is this place? It's not my neighborhood. It doesn't look familiar at all!"

Rajesh stared at her, open-mouthed. "But, this is where you and I have been walking regularly for the past month!"

She stared back at him. A look of fear crossed her face, and she shrank back. Her voice trembling, she said, "What do you mean, we have been walking here together regularly? Who *are* you?"

"Don't you remember me?" exclaimed Rajesh.

"No, I have never seen you before," she replied, anxiety now replacing her fear. "Am I supposed to know you?"

Rajesh, with a horrified feeling of *deja vu*, began to realize what had happened. The blow from the hard cricket ball, striking Geetha on her head, appeared to have wiped out her recent memories! Now she did not even recognize who he was. Anguish welled up within him, but he controlled himself with an effort.

One of the boys standing around them spoke up. "But, auntie! We have seen you and uncle walking around here often, in the evenings!"

She stared at the boy, then at Rajesh. Her eyes filled with tears. "What are you all saying? I don't remember anything like that!"

"Geetha —" began Rajesh.

"And why do you keep calling me Geetha? My name isn't Geetha — it's Uma!"

"You remember your name!" exclaimed Rajesh.

She stared at him, a flush coming to her cheeks. "Of course I remember my name! Why wouldn't I?"

39

"But you don't remember living with me for the past month?" he asked, anguish in his voice.

Her eyes widened and she looked at him as though he had lost his mind.

"Living with you?" she gasped. "But I live with my aunt and uncle!" She started crying, then burst out hysterically: "I don't know why you're saying such things! I've never seen you before!"

Rajesh's gazed at her helplessly. The latest blow on Geetha/Uma's head appeared to have restored the memories of her life prior to her accident a month ago, but had at the same time perversely wiped out all the memories formed after the accident. So now she had no recollection of living in his flat, and was unable to even recognize him!

A sense of despair swept over Rajesh — fate was indeed cruelly toying with him. How could he even begin to tell her about the prior bad hit and run accident that had wiped out all memories of her past, and how he had brought her to his flat to live with him and his mother?

Just then, they heard a hoarse shout, and looking up, saw a portly, middle aged man running towards them as fast as he could. When he came closer, he cried out, "Uma!"

"Uncle!" cried Uma. She tried to stand up, staggered and almost fell. Rajesh moved swiftly to her side and supported her.

The stranger drew up, panting. "Oh, my God, Uma, I've finally found you! We've been nearly losing our minds over the past month, not knowing where you were..."

"Uncle!" cried Uma again. She stepped forward and

collapsed against him. "Uncle, I am so glad to see you! I don't know what I am doing here — I am so scared! Please take me home, Uncle!"

Her uncle put his arms around her and said soothingly, "Yes, yes, of course, *beti*. I am going to take you home." He turned his head to eye Rajesh suspiciously and demanded, "What happened to my niece?"

"She was struck on the head by a cricket ball..." was all Rajesh could think of saying. He felt like events were moving too fast for him. He gestured towards the group of schoolboys standing around them, silently watching the drama unfold. "These boys were playing cricket nearby, and the ball came flying through the air, and struck her on her temple..."

"Oh, my God!" the uncle exclaimed.

Uma put a hand to her temple and winced. "It hurts!"

"She actually lost consciousness for a few minutes," Rajesh added. "I really think, sir, that she should be taken to a hospital immediately, so that they can run tests to ensure that she doesn't have a concussion."

"You think so?" asked Uma's uncle doubtfully. "Well, we'll see..."

"Sir, I am a doctor," Rajesh said, desperately. "So please trust me when I say that it needs to be done right away."

"A doctor, eh?" the uncle's attitude became much more friendly. "You really think I should take her to a hospital?"

"Yes — AIIMS Hospital is not that far away," Rajesh said. "Please let me call for an ambulance."

"I'll take her there in my car," Uma's uncle said. "I

know where it is, and it would be faster than waiting for an ambulance. How do you feel, my dear — do you feel well enough to walk to my car?"

"Yes, uncle."

Uma's uncle turned to Rajesh and said, "Thank you, doctor, for your help. I'll take care of my niece now."

As they walked away, he could hear Uma saying, "It's so odd, uncle — that young man was calling me by a different name, and saying such strange things…"

"There, there, my dear, you're safe now…"

Rajesh watched them go, anguish in his heart, but feeling powerless to stop them.

He became aware that the boys were still standing around, staring at him silently. Had they grasped what had just happened, or were they too young to understand? Perhaps some of them had understood, for he saw sympathy on some of the faces. But Rajesh didn't know what to say to them. What could he say?

He hung his head and turned away. The boys looked at each other, shrugged, and returned to their cricket game.

Rajesh couldn't for the life of him remember how he managed to walk back home that evening. His mind a maelstrom of confused thoughts, his legs moved robotically, with some innate instinct directing his way. Eventually he arrived back at his flat and let himself in. His mother, who was sitting in the living room watching TV, looked up, took one look at his ashen face, and struggled to her feet. She cried: "Rajesh *beta*, why are you looking like this? What happened?" She peered past him and cried: "Where is Geetha?"

He collapsed into her arms, put his head on her shoulder, and began to sob uncontrollably. "She's gone, mother! She's gone..."

§

The subsequent days and weeks were like a never ending nightmare for Rajesh. Although there had always been the thought at the back of his mind that Geetha's memory might be restored someday, and she would leave his home to return to her former life, he had never imagined that it would happen in this fashion, where her memories of him would be wiped out, and she wouldn't even know who he was. The very thought of her brought a dull ache to his heart. He tried his best to carry on with his work and life as usual, but he could not fight off the constant feeling that there was now a gaping void in his life. He threw himself into his work, deliberately working extra hours to the point of exhaustion, so that his mind would be numb by the time he returned home.

One day some two weeks later, it was his day off from work, and Rajesh went out to get a haircut and do some shopping. When he returned back home and was unlocking and opening the front door of his flat, he heard the sound of voices coming from inside. *Some neighbors must have dropped in to chat with Mother*, he thought. He was glad, because she too had been very depressed ever since the girl they had named Geetha had disappeared from their lives.

When he stepped into his living room, he stopped and stared, hardly able to believe his eyes. Seated there, and talking to his mother, was Geetha, or rather, Uma (which was her real name, he had to remind himself) and her uncle.

Uma jumped to her feet and came towards him.

"Rajesh!" she cried.

Rajesh stared at her helplessly, tongue-tied with surprise. His heart was thumping madly in his chest and he felt short of breath.

"Rajesh, I am *so* sorry for going away like that with my uncle that evening — I just could not remember who you were then!" she said, her voice choked with tears. "Later, my memories of you began to come back, and I began to recall how I was in a hospital after a bad accident, and how you much you helped me there, and how you brought me to your flat to live with you and your mother rather than being sent to a women's shelter or orphanage. I began to recall how you both took such good care of me, and how you both treated me as part of the family ..." Her words came tumbling out in a torrent, and tears were running down her face.

She paused for breath, and continued: "But even as my memories of living with you started coming back, I still couldn't recall your phone number or address, so I didn't know how to contact you. Then my uncle suggested that we look at a map of the areas surrounding the park where he had found me. When I looked at the map, the Hauz Khas Apartments seemed very familiar. So we came over all the way from where we lived in Mukherjee Nagar, on the opposite end of town, and the guard at the gate here recognized me and recalled that he had seen me with you often and told us which flat you lived in. Your mother was so glad to see me! She has been telling me how depressed you have been ever since I left."

She took another hesitant step towards him, and said softly, "Coming back to this neighborhood brought back my memories of how you and I used to take long walks together in the evenings, talking about whatever came to our minds —" She was now smiling tremulously at him through her tears, her bright eyes looking like twin stars. She had come up very close to him.

Before he fully realized what he was doing, Rajesh held out his arms and Uma, with a little cry of happiness, stepped into them. He hugged her tight, oblivious to everyone else in the room, feeling only her presence as she laid her head on his chest, her tears dripping on to his shirt. He whispered hoarsely, "I've missed you so much! I love you, Uma. I don't want to ever lose you again."

And he heard her whisper softly, "You won't lose me ever again, I promise."

The Formidable Mr. Shah

When Dorothy came out of Mr. Shah's office, closing the door behind her — Mr. Shah, our Office Manager, always liked to keep his door closed — and started walking slowly back to her desk, I didn't pay much attention at first. Dorothy D'Souza was one of the oldest employees in our office, a diminutive, gray-haired lady with a sharp, intelligent face. I had noticed that she had been summoned to Mr. Shah's office, but that in itself wasn't unusual; he once in a while summoned one of the senior clerks into his office to discuss who knows what weighty matters — junior clerks like myself were not privy to those discussions.

When Dorothy came out of Mr. Shah's office I was seated at my desk, staring hard at the computer screen in front of me, concentrating on making sure that I was entering data correctly, for Mr. Shah hated mistakes of any kind, and he was constantly monitoring our work. There were six of us clerks in that office, and together we formed the centralized Clearing Department of the large bank that we were part of.

I disliked Mr. Shah, and I think this feeling was shared by many of the other clerks. He seldom spoke to any of us. When he entered the outer office in the morning, at precisely 9:30 am every day, he would majestically walk up the broad aisle in between the two rows of identical desks where we clerks sat and did our work, to his private office behind an ominous green door. He always looked straight ahead and never to the right or left, and never said a word to any one of us, not even a civil "Good morning". He would then unlock and enter his private office, and close the door firmly. We would typically not see him again until lunchtime, when at 1:00 pm precisely, the door to his office would open, and he would proceed along the aisle to the outer door of our office, and disappear for an hour. He would return at exactly 2:00 pm, go into his private office, close the door and would not be seen again until 5:30 in the evening, when he would leave the office until the next morning. This was Mr. Shah's daily unvarying routine. When he wished to speak to one of us, he would call that person on the telephone, summon the person into his den, and meet with him or her behind closed doors.

Some of the junior clerks (myself included) joked that Mr. Shah went to sleep in his office every day, only waking up to go to lunch at mid-day and to go home in the evening. But we were all careful not to say such things when he was around, even if he was behind the closed door in his office, for we were all quite scared of Mr. Shah. There was something very intimidating about him.

But to return to the events of that day when Dorothy was summoned to Mr. Shah's private office: after she came out and returned to her desk, some instinct made me look away from my computer screen and towards her. To my surprise, I saw that Dorothy was taking out her personal belongings from the drawers of her desk. All of us kept some of our personal stuff in our desk drawers, although strictly speaking, we were not supposed to. She was putting them into a cardboard box, and tears were running down her cheeks.

I got up and walked over to her. "Dorothy, what's wrong? Why are you crying and cleaning out your desk?"

She looked up and said, choking and barely able to get the words out: "I've been let go, *beta*."

My mouth dropped open in astonishment. Dorothy had worked here the longest, longer than even Mr. Shah. She was such a fixture in that office that I found it hard to believe what I had just heard. Some of the other clerks in the office had stopped working and were staring in our direction.

"What do you mean, let go?" I asked. "You mean you're sacked?"

Dorothy nodded. "I won't be working here anymore."

Now that it was beginning to sink in, I felt a stirring of anger. "But he can't do that!" I said, referring, of course, to Mr. Shah. "Why, you're the best clerk in this office!" Which was true: despite her age, Dorothy had a sharp memory and knew exactly where everything was filed. She was also a very conscientious worker, usually the first to arrive and the last to leave.

"It's all right, *beta*." She tried to smile bravely through her tears.

"No, it's not all right!" I exclaimed. I pointed at the green door of Mr. Shah's office. "I am going to go in there and tell Mr. Shah that he can't do this to you." My anger was making me reckless. But then, I've always been somewhat headstrong.

There was also another reason why I was so upset that Dorothy was being let go. When I had joined the department some six months ago, fresh out of college, Dorothy was the one who had very kindly taken me under her wing and patiently trained me how to do my job. I have always been grateful to her for that.

I marched along the aisle to the ominous green door behind which sat an equally ominous Mr. Shah. All the other employees in the office were now staring at me. Two of the older ones shook their heads, as if to say, "Don't be foolish. Don't risk your job." But the younger clerks gave me a big thumbs up and grinned.

I knocked on the door to Mr. Shah's office, and entered without waiting for his reply. I closed the door and strode up to his large desk.

All manner of files and reports covered his desk, and he had been poring over a computer spreadsheet when I made my sudden entrance. He looked up from the report he had been studying, frowned at me, and said, "Oh, it's you, Raj. What is it? I don't recall calling you and asking you to come see me."

I must say, I was surprised when he addressed me by my name. I had thought that we were all nameless entities to him.

I drew a deep breath and plunged right in. "Sir, you can't let Dorothy D'Souza go! She's one of the best employees you have! She knows our files and our Accounts better than anyone."

Mr. Shah leaned back in his chair, the frown on his face deepening. He said, "I am the manager of this department. I don't have to explain my actions to you."

I didn't say anything, just stood there in front of him. There was silence for a few minutes, only broken by the distant sounds of Mumbai traffic coming in through the open window, from the street down far below our floor.

After frowning at me for a few moments, Mr. Shah said: "Did Mrs. D'Souza tell you, or any of the others, why she was being let go?"

"No, sir. All she said was that she wouldn't be working here anymore."

"I see. Well, in that case, perhaps I should explain. It took a lot of courage for you to come in here and speak up on her behalf, so it's perhaps only fair that you should know. Also, the other clerks may feel the same way you do, and I do not wish to hurt the morale of the department. Oh, I am well aware that you fellows gossip! So when they question you later — and I am sure they will be bristling with curiosity — you can apprise them of the facts."

He paused and continued: "The bank's profits are down sharply this year. Two days ago, I was notified by senior management that cutbacks had to be made throughout the bank, and I had to let go of one person in this department. They left it up to me to decide who it should be."

Mr. Shah paused once again, and said: "Believe me, it wasn't easy to decide who to let go. I reviewed all the employee files, and then decided on Dorothy D'Souza."

"But why her, sir?" I blurted out.

He seemed to be on the verge of telling me that it was none of my business, then appeared to change his mind, and said: "Were you aware that Mrs. D'Souza, because of her age, is only six months away from mandatory retirement?"

I hadn't known that, so I replied quite honestly, "No, sir, I didn't."

"Ah!" said Mr. Shah. "So she would have had to retire after six months, anyway. Due to her long years of service here, she will be receiving a nice early retirement package and a pension." Mr. Shah paused to let this all sink in. Then he added, "There's something else that you may not know. She is widowed and lives with her son, who has a good job – as a matter of fact, he too works for the bank. So I don't think she will have any financial difficulties."

I didn't know what to say. I just stood there, beginning to feel somewhat foolish.

Mr. Shah then said, a faint smile coming to his lips: "But since you feel so strongly that Mrs. D'Souza should be retained, I'll have to let someone else go in her place." He made a show of pondering, rubbing his chin and leaning back in his chair. "Now let's see, who should it be? You have the least amount of tenure here, since you started just six months ago. Perhaps I should lay you off in place of Dorothy D'Souza?"

I gulped, and said hurriedly, "Mr. Shah, I assure you, I don't feel bad about Dorothy being let go anymore! I can see now that she was the best choice. I will explain to the rest of the office, if anyone asks. Sorry I bothered you, sir."

"Very good. Now get back to work."

As I stumbled out of the room, I swear that I heard Mr. Shah give forth a loud chuckle. And had there not been a twinkle in his eyes when he had talked about letting me go in place of Dorothy?

At that moment, I realized that my dislike of Mr. Shah had vanished.

The Thunderstorm

The rain began quite suddenly. It had been sunny all morning, but after lunch, dark clouds gathered with a speed which astonished everyone and caught them unprepared, since it wasn't the monsoon season. When the big fat drops of water began coming down, it sent the people on the street scurrying to and fro seeking shelter, for most of them had come out without their umbrellas.

Sen was one of those it caught unprepared. When the first raindrops hit him, he quickened his pace along the narrow street, but when the rain started coming down in force, he made a dash for the nearest shelter he could find: a small porch with an overhanging roof, jutting out in front of the door of a rather old house. The concrete porch could not have been more than five feet in length and couple of feet in width, but the roof over it provided some measure of protection from the downpour.

Sen had no sooner gained access to the porch than another man came dashing up. Sen moved to one side to allow the stranger access to the shelter. The new arrival was a plump middle-aged man of medium height, well dressed in a dark coat and tan slacks.

The stranger took out a white handkerchief from his trouser pocket and wiped his face.

"Now, who would have thought it would rain today!" he remarked.

"And it doesn't look like it will stop anytime soon," Sen responded. Indeed, by now the rain was coming down in sheets, and dark clouds filled the entire sky. The street in front of them had become filled with gushing water. A car went splashing by slowly, its windshield wipers working furiously against the downpour.

Sen felt some drops of water fall on his head, and glanced upwards. The termite-ridden beams of the old roof above them was seeping with moisture. A few drops fell on the older man's head, and he shrank back against the weatherbeaten wooden door behind the small porch.

"Doesn't look like we chose the best place to take shelter in," Sen said.

"Any port in a storm," his companion responded, smiling wryly.

They stood in silence for few minutes, during which the thunderstorm continued unabated. Two men went by on bicycles, grim faced, drenched to the skin, but pedaling away furiously. Sen liked their attitude. At least they were getting somewhere!

Drops were now falling on them regularly from the moisture filled roof. The upper portion of Sen's shirt had become quite wet.

Sen suddenly made up his mind. "I'm going to get out of here," he said to his companion.

The other man gave him a startled glance. "But the rain is pretty bad."

"I'm getting wet standing here, anyway," argued Sen.

"But not as wet as you'll get if you were to go out there," his older companion responded.

"Do you think the rain will stop in the next ten to

fifteen minutes?" demanded Sen.

"Doesn't look like it."

"Then it's silly to stand here like this," Sen said. He felt himself getting irritated by his companion. That was the problem with older people, he thought. Their logic was beyond him. What was the point of standing there when the roof above them was leaking and they were getting more and more wet?

Sen had initially thought he and the other man, despite their differences in age, had something in common. They had both been caught by this sudden thunderstorm, and taken shelter under the same roof. But now it was becoming clear to him that there was a vast difference in the way they thought. It looked like the other was willing to stand under a leaky roof all afternoon long, hoping the rain would stop! This attitude annoyed Sen immensely, just like how his own father's attitude annoyed him often.

Sen spotted a cafe on the opposite side of the street, a bit further down. He could go over there, sit under the fan, and order a hot *chai* and some snacks. In no time at all, his clothes would be dry. Even if his clothes didn't dry out completely, it was far better than waiting under this leaky roof.

Sen turned to his companion. "Well, I'm not going to stay here a minute longer. I'm leaving."

"As you wish," the other replied, smiling.

That smile was the final straw. Sen squared his shoulders and dashed out into the downpour. He didn't look back once. By the time he reached the cafe, he was completely drenched. But he didn't care. He slid into a comfortable booth, and mopped his face with his handkerchief.

A waiter came up and took his order. Sen leaned back and savored the aroma of spicy tea and fried food that permeated the small restaurant. The booths and tables around him were filled with people drinking cups of hot *chai* and talking animatedly with one another. Ah! Now this was far better than where he had been standing, getting slowly but inexorably soaked.

That is what one needs to do — take swift and bold action when it was necessary, thought Sen. He thought contemptuously of his former middle-aged companion. That was the problem with the older generation — they had no spirit of adventure, they were just content to just plod along in their existence, never taking any risks, never really *living* life, so to speak.

The waiter brought him his tea and a plate containing two golden brown *samosas*. Sen took a sip of the milky-sweet aromatic spiced tea, and a bite out of one of the plump *samosas,* and sighed contentedly. If one takes bold action, one can reap the rewards.

"So there you are, my young friend!" he heard someone say.

Sen looked up. It was his erstwhile companion from the leaky porch. He then noticed that the rain had stopped, and the street outside the cafe was again full of pedestrians.

"Mind if I join you?" the man asked. He held a cup of steaming *chai* in his hand.

Sen nodded, reluctantly.

The older man squeezed into the booth, seating himself across the table. He took a sip of his chai, smiled indulgently and said, "You were in too much of a hurry, for the rain stopped just ten minutes after you left."

Sen felt his annoyance return. "And what if it hadn't?" he snapped.

The older man shrugged. "It would have stopped, eventually. These kinds of thunderstorms don't last forever, you know, especially since it's not the monsoon season."

"Well, I didn't want to waste any more time waiting," Sen said. "At times, bold action is needed. But you appear to have a very different temperament."

"Oh, its not that," his companion responded. He patted the left side of his coat. "I am carrying some very important documents in my inside coat pocket. I couldn't afford to let them get drenched. They are originals, you see, with original seals and signatures, and it would be very difficult to replace them. I knew that if I walked out into the downpour, like you did, the documents would be ruined. I felt that I had a better chance of keeping them safe by staying on that porch, even if the roof leaked a bit." He finished his tea, extracted his wallet, and put some rupee notes on the table. "Anyway, I've got to go. I was on my way to deliver the documents to my bank when I got caught in that thunderstorm."

After the stranger had left, Sen sat staring into space, absentmindedly finishing up the rest of the *samosas* and drinking his *chai*. He pulled out his mobile phone, called his father, and spoke very nicely to him, much to that old man's surprise and delight.

The Girl He Spent the Night With

In the heart of New Delhi stands one of the most famous landmarks in the city, India Gate. Although built almost a century ago, it has been well preserved and does not show its age. Surrounding this monument are a number of beautiful green parks filled with shady trees and man-made pools of water. These parks are a popular spot for the residents of the city; the tourists mainly congregate around the monument itself.

In one such park, a young couple sat on a stone bench under a shady tree, facing a large, rectangular pool. It was an evening in early summer, and the air was beginning to cool after the heat of the day, but still held a languid warmth.

The girl was very pretty, with classic features, dark hair that fell around her shoulders, and large almond-shaped eyes. Despite the beauty of the evening and the surroundings, her face wore a look of deep sadness. The young man seated by her was short but well-built, and he was staring moodily, almost savagely, across the water.

Just a few minutes earlier, he had asked the girl to marry him, and had been rejected.

He turned back to her. "Won't you think it over?"

"I shall never marry," she replied. "You know why."

"Because of Vikram?" he asked, bitterly.

"Yes. I will always love him."

The young man burst out, petulantly: "But Vikram is dead! Gone! Granted, he died a hero's death, bravely fighting enemy soldiers in the mountains of Kashmir, but he's never coming back."

"Yes, I know," she whispered. Tears were beginning to form in her eyes.

"You cannot say that you will never marry! It's absurd. You are still young, and you have your whole life ahead of you."

"It doesn't matter," the girl said softly.

The young man turned his face away and again stared moodily across the water. That's when the temptation came to him. Should he tell her what he knew? Perhaps he should. What was that old saying? 'All's fair in love and war'.

He turned back to her. "Maya, what I am about to tell you I do for your sake. You will probably think that I'm a cad, but I'm going to take the risk."

The girl turned her head sideways to look at him,

puzzled. "What on earth are you talking about?"

"You know that Vikram and I were good friends?" the young man asked.

"Of course," she replied.

He turned his face away from her and stared ahead, at the water. "I know that Vikram was not faithful to you."

The girl stared at him, a flush coming to her cheeks. The young man refused to meet her gaze. Hands clasped and head bowed, his gaze was fixed on the ground.

"Why are you saying such things?" she demanded, angrily. "It isn't nice."

The young man took a deep breath, and still refusing to meet her indignant gaze, said: "The last night Vikram spent here in New Delhi, before he left with his Mountain Division for Kashmir – he spent that night at a hotel with a girl."

There was a silence. Then the girl said, in a low, husky voice: "Why are you telling me this?"

"To make you understand that he was no saint. Oh, there's no doubt that he was a brave soldier, and acted with heroism and courage. But he had his weaknesses, like other men." He paused, and continued: "Perhaps you'll now see that the ideal you have conjured up was no ideal. My point is, since he wasn't faithful to you, you shouldn't remain faithful to his memory and throw your life away for him."

There was another silence. Then she shook her head and said, with tears in her eyes, "I still love him."

The young man now raised his head and turned to her, indignantly. "Even after what I just told you?"

"Yes. You see, I know he spent that last night here in

Delhi with a girl."

The young man stared at her, open-mouthed. "You knew? And you still say that you love him?"

"Yes," she replied. Her eyes were now shining brightly through her tears, and there was a half-smile upon her lips. She said softly, "The girl with whom he spent that night…"

"Yes?"

"I was that girl. I was the girl he spent the night with."

The Storyteller

I found myself suddenly thinking of Mr. Rao, and my memories took me back to when I was a young boy growing up in a small town in southern India in the early 1960's. He lived in our neighborhood, and me and my two best friends, Kothand and Arbi, were in the habit of going over to his house in the evenings, to sit on his veranda and listen to him tell us stories. He was a short, plump man, with a round, moonlike face and a bald head circled by a fringe of white hair. He was a gifted raconteur and he would sit comfortably in his easy chair, hands folded across his plump stomach, and hold the three of us spell-bound with adventurous tales of far-off lands.

Mr. Rao lived in a little bungalow with a covered veranda in front, which looked out over a neatly kept little garden. It was peaceful to sit there in the evening's fading sunlight and listen to his stories. An added attraction was that his wife — a short, plump lady, built very much like him — would usually bring out a plate of biscuits or some other snacks for us to munch on. They lived alone; they had a daughter who, after her marriage, had gone to live with her husband in another town.

Mr. Rao would often say that his biggest asset was his vivid imagination, which enabled him to concoct the stories that he narrated to us. And vanity aside, he seemed to truly enjoy our company. We must have comprised a delightful audience, hanging on to his every word and giving him our spontaneous admiration. He was kind enough to say that our presence spurred his fertile imagination to new, creative heights.

During these story-telling sessions, Mr. Rao was in the habit of dropping mysterious hints about a great novel that he was working on. He frequently asserted that ever since he had retired a few years previously, he had the time to fulfill his ambition of turning out a worthy and abiding literary piece of work, a book through which he could freely express his thoughts and ideas. As far as we could tell, this novel of his had been in progress for several years and would be, he promised us, "epic".

Naturally, me and my two friends were filled with curiosity. Wouldn't he tell us something about the book? But no matter how much we pleaded, he would never reveal the plot, nor the theme, nor anything else, about what he had written thus far.

§

One day during the summer holidays, a cousin of Arbi's, by name Indira, came to stay with his family for a few weeks. This Indira was actually a first year in college, and therefore much older than we were: Kothand, Arbi, and I were all just twelve years old at the time.

Indira was a proud, haughty girl and very much aware that she was in college, while we were all, as she termed it, "little schoolboys". But there were few girls of her own age in the neighborhood, so she ended up spending a fair amount of time with us.

"Where do you boys dash off to every evening?" she

asked. "I see all three of you going off, looking very mysterious."

"Oh!" said Arbi. "We go to Mr. Rao's house."

"And who is this Mr. Rao?"

"He's an old chap who lives a couple of streets away."

"Why do you like going to see him?" asked Indira.

"He tells us stories," Arbi said.

"Really wonderful tales!" I put in.

"We love sitting on his veranda and listening to him," Kothand said.

Indira looked interested. "A story-teller! That's becoming a lost art, you know. In ancient days, many of our famous epics, like the Ramayana and the Mahabharata, were actually verbally narrated by sages before they were written down. Not that you boys would know anything of that," she added, disparagingly.

"Of course we've heard of the Ramayana and the Mahabharata!" I retorted hotly, stung by the girl's condescending manner.

"Ah, but I bet you didn't know that they were originally narrated by ancient sages to their disciples!" said Indira, looking smug.

The three of us glanced at each other, then admitted, albeit reluctantly, that we had not known that.

"Anyway," Indira added. "I would like to come with you boys one evening and meet this Mr. Rao."

We glanced at each other again, this time uneasily. I knew what was in each of our minds: did we want to expose nice Mr. Rao to this arrogant girl? What if she were to make fun of his story-telling and insult him? We sort of felt proprietary towards the old man and didn't want to cause him any distress.

But ultimately, we were unable come up with a good enough excuse as to why Indira couldn't accompany us to Mr. Rao's house. She brushed aside the few weak objections that we were able to articulate.

So, one evening, she accompanied us when we went to visit Mr. Rao. He was, as usual, seated on his veranda, and was glad to see us.

"Hullo, boys!" he called out as we entered through his front gate and walked up the path that led through his garden. He peered benevolently at Indira, and said, "Ah, I see that I have a new visitor! Welcome, my dear. And what is your name?"

"Indira, sir," she replied politely, smiling at him.

Arbi, Kothand and I glanced at each other, surprised. We had not known that Indira could be capable of such politeness.

"She is my cousin, uncle," Arbi explained. "She's visiting us for a few weeks."

"Excellent!" Mr. Rao said. "Sit wherever you want, boys, as you usually do. Would you like a chair to sit on, my dear?" he asked Indira.

"No need, uncle. I'll be happy to sit on the veranda itself, like the others," she replied. And she promptly squatted down, cross-legged, at his feet.

Wonder of wonders — this was indeed a new and different Indira!

"Are you in school, Indira, like these young friends of mine?" asked Mr. Rao.

"I am in my first year of college," replied Indira, proudly.

"Indeed! And what is your major field of study?"

"I am working towards a Bachelor of Arts degree in Literature, uncle."

Mr. Rao's eyes lit up. "That is simply marvellous!" he cried, beaming all over his round face. "I, too, am very fond of literature, as these boys might have told you."

"They told me that you are a gifted story-teller, uncle."

"Pshaw!" Mr. Rao said modestly, waving a plump hand in the air. "They flatter me." Lowering his voice, he added, conspiratorially, "I am also writing a novel, you know."

"Why, uncle, that is wonderful!" Indira exclaimed. "What is it about?"

"Ah, my dear, I cannot reveal that," said Mr. Rao, laughing and shaking his head. "My young friends have tried often enough, but I have been able to staunchly resist their entreaties thus far."

I was looking at Indira as he said this, to see how she would react. With a sinking feeling, I recognized the expression that came over her face at that moment: the look of one who has been thrown a gauntlet, and decided to accept the challenge.

"Oh, Mr. Rao, surely you must tell me more!" she cried. "Don't send me away empty-handed in regards to your book! Couldn't you narrate a chapter, or if a chapter is too much, at least a passage?"

At this point, I should in all fairness reveal that Indira, despite her lofty manner towards us boys, was actually a very attractive young lady. Mr. Rao was being subject to the full force of her charming face, bright eyes, and caressing voice.

Mr. Rao tried vainly to resist, but his defenses were no match for her. He eventually succumbed. Well then, he would quote a passage from his monumental work.

At the end of his narration, we boys broke into spontaneous applause. Indira clapped politely, but there was in her eyes a gleam which made me distinctly uneasy. I don't know if my two friends noticed it.

Soon afterwards, we took our leave, and began walking homewards. Indira seemed to be very pleased with herself, humming a light tune as she walked along.

Finally, Arbi said, "That was excellent, wasn't it, the paragraph that Mr. Rao narrated from his novel?"

Indira looked at him and laughed.

"My dear cousin!" she said in the pitying tone she usually adopted when talking to us. "Have any of you read 'A Passage to India' by E.M. Forster?"

We said no, we hadn't.

"Read it. Then the excerpt that Mr. Rao narrated, supposedly from his novel, will seem extraordinarily familiar."

Arbi frowned. "What are you driving at, Indira? Are you saying that Mr. Rao has copied from this book you just mentioned?"

"I believe the term is *plagiarize*," Indira said. She wore the self-satisfied, righteous look of a teacher who has manged to catch one of her students red-handed in the act of copying from his neighbor.

We looked at one another, thunderstruck. Surely our

nice Mr. Rao, with whom we had spent many a pleasant evening, couldn't be capable of this!

"Indira, you must be mistaken!" cried Arbi.

Indira shook her head, smugly. "If you happen to have a copy of 'A Passage to India' at home, I'll show you the excerpt. If you don't have it at home, let's go to the local library. They're bound to have it there, and I'll prove to you that I'm right."

We walked on in silence. A chill had fallen upon the company. The three of us couldn't even bear to look at each other. Indira strode on ahead, humming a light tune again.

For about a week after that, although we met as usual, we avoided going to Mr. Rao's house. Neither did any of us bring up his name.

But something was gnawing at the back of my mind: the twinkle I had seen in Mr. Rao's eyes before he narrated the excerpt from his novel.

One evening, I decided to go and see Mr. Rao. I went by myself, because I wished to find out the truth, and I did not wish to explain to the others, especially to Indira, why I wanted to talk to Mr. Rao.

I found him seated as usual on his veranda. As I entered through his front gate, he called out, "My young friend, it is so nice to see you again! I was afraid that you boys had quite forgotten me." I detected a note of sadness in his voice.

"I'm sorry that we've not been coming, uncle." I walked up and sat down in my usual spot on the veranda, facing Mr. Rao and leaning my back against one of the concrete columns that supported the sloping tiled roof overhead.

"What have you and your two friends been doing with yourselves?" he asked. "Got tired of my stories, eh?"

I hesitated. How should I bring up what had happened the last time we had met with him here? Then I decided to take the bull by the horns. Taking a deep breath, I said: "Uncle, to be quite honest, that passage you narrated from the novel that you're writing..."

Mr. Rao's reaction startled me. He threw back his head and laughed uproariously. He laughed till tears ran down his cheeks and his face grew red, his plump body shaking like jelly.

"Oh dear, oh dear," he finally said, wiping the tears from his eyes. "I should have known that would get me in trouble!"

"What do you mean, uncle?"

"That passage I narrated, supposedly from my novel? It wasn't from my novel at all! It was from another book, one called 'A Passage to India' by E.M. Forster."

Hope was beginning to dawn on me. I waited for him to go on.

"You see, I wanted to pull that young lady's leg. Now, what was her name – Indira?"

"Yes."

"Indira was so sure of herself, so confident that she could work her feminine wiles to make me do something that I have resisted doing for many years – that is, reveal a part of my novel. It became a battle of wits. It was very naughty of me, I know, but I couldn't help but to try and prick her pride a bit. I fully expected her to denounce me on the spot, and angrily declare that the excerpt I had narrated was from a fairly well-known classic, since she is, after all, studying Literature in college. When she didn't, I was somewhat nonplussed, I admit."

At that point, I told him about how Indira had jumped to the conclusion that he was actually plagiarizing from another work.

"Oh, dear!" Mr. Rao said, his expression becoming serious. "I would not wish her − or anybody else, for that matter − to think that. Will you please explain to her that I was just playing a joke?"

"I will, uncle," I said. "To be honest, my friends are going to be very relieved when they hear this. Indira had convinced us that you were copying from some other author's work. That's why we all stopped coming; we felt very awkward about seeing you after that."

Mr. Rao now looked genuinely distressed. "I certainly did not want that to happen! I really enjoy having you boys come over − it was something I looked forward to every evening. Please tell your friends, and Indira too, that I apologize for the little joke I played on you all."

"I will go and tell them right away, uncle," I said, and took my leave.

My friends were extremely relieved when I recounted my conversation with Mr. Rao. Not so Indira. We could tell that she was really miffed at having her leg pulled in this fashion.

"Well, it's your fault, Indira," Arbi said. "You pestered him to reveal a part of his novel, so in order to pacify you, he quoted from another book instead."

"I think it was rather mean," Indira huffed.

"Actually, Mr. Rao said that it had developed into a battle of wits between the two of you," I said. "He actually expected you to recognize the excerpt he had narrated, and denounce him on the spot."

"Did he, indeed?" Indira said, with a slight softening of manner.

"Yes. And he said that he apologized most profusely for the little joke he played on all of us, and he is hoping that we will resume going to his place."

"We will definitely do so," my two friends chorused.

§

Several years passed by. My friends and I were now in high school, and consequently very busy with our studies, and our visits to Mr. Rao's house became more and more infrequent. Eventually, I ended up going out of town to study at a well known university in a larger city some two hundred miles away. My two close friends also left the small town we had all grown up in: Kothand went to an Engineering college in another town, while Arbi chose to study Accounting elsewhere.

One summer, when I had returned home for the holidays, I decided to look up Mr. Rao and see how he was doing. I had thought of him from time to time while I was away at the university.

Upon arriving at his little bungalow, I was surprised to see that he was not seated on the veranda as usual. With a sense of foreboding, I walked up the gravel path and knocked on the front door. It was opened by Mrs. Rao. I was shocked to see how old and faded she looked.

"Hello, Mrs. Rao," I said.

She looked at me tiredly, then recognition slowly

dawned in her eyes.

"Oh – you are one of the boys who used to come and sit with my husband in the evenings when you were all young, aren't you?"

"Yes," I replied. "I would like to say hello to him, if I may."

Her eyes filled with tears. "He passed away just three weeks ago."

I stood there, numb. I had not expected this. Finally I said, "I am so sorry. Please accept my condolences."

"Thank you. Please do come in," Mrs. Rao said. She stepped back and indicated an armchair in their small living room. After I had seated myself, she sat down on a small sofa across from me and said: "He had been ailing for some time. He had grown very out of shape from lack of exercise – he liked nothing better than to sit and read and write all day long. All that inactivity resulted in a host of ailments: high blood pressure, diabetes, heart disease, and so on."

I didn't know what to say. After a pause of a few minutes, I said, awkwardly, "I am sorry to hear of his ill health. I thought of him often, you know."

"That was nice of you," Mrs. Rao said, with a faint smile. "You must have been busy, otherwise you would have come by, at least once in a while."

I explained to her that I had gone to a university out of town. "I'm studying for a Bachelors Degree in Literature," I added. "I think Mr. Rao inspired me to major in that field."

Her face lit up. "He would have been very pleased to hear that."

"Did he manage to finish his novel?" I asked. "The one that he had been working on for so many years?"

Mrs. Rao shook her head. "No, he never did. After a certain point, he became too ill to continue his writing." She stood up and said, "Come, I want to show you something."

She led the way into another small room whose windows faced the front garden. The small room was crammed with books: tall bookcases filled to bursting point lined the walls, and there were piles of books on the floor. The room had the woody, earthy, musty smell that one associates with libraries, a smell that I've always loved.

At one end of the room, by the window, stood a heavy wooden desk. On it was a tall bundle of paper, tied up with string. Mrs. Rao walked over and rested a plump hand on the bundle.

"This is it," she said. "This is his unfinished novel."

A sudden idea seized me. Surprised at my own boldness, I asked, "May I have it?"

Mrs. Rao looked at the stack of manuscript, then back at me, and said: "I don't see why not. In all honesty, I wouldn't know what to do with it — I have never been much of a reader, and it would intimidate me to tackle such a huge piece of work. In a way, it's probably fitting that you should have it, since you and your friends gave him so much pleasure, visiting him in the evenings and listening to his stories. He really enjoyed all that, you know. He did not have many friends, since he was such a bookworm. He was a lonely man."

"Thank you very much, Mrs. Rao." I lifted up the bundle of papers and tucked it under my arm. "This means a great deal to me."

As I walked back home, I felt like I was carrying a treasure. Mr. Rao had dropped so many hints about his monumental work, without revealing any details, and I now actually had it in my hands. My plan was to read his novel, and perhaps attempt to finish it, if I could in a manner that would do justice to what he had already penned. I would then try my best to get it published under his name.

I think Mr. Rao, wherever he is, would like that.

The Muse

"Uncle! Did you know that there's a dog following you?"

The Music Teacher stopped and peered suspiciously at the group of four young schoolboys standing by the roadside under the shade of a large tree.

"What did you say?" he asked the boy who had called out to him. He was the tallest of the group and appeared to be their leader.

"There's a dog following you, uncle," replied the boy. He pointed. "Look! There he is, right behind you."

The Music Teacher turned around. Sure enough, there was a dog behind him. But this was not one of those ordinary flea-bitten, mangy strays that could be seen roaming the streets all over town and congregating in the marketplaces. Rather, it was a beautiful dog, very clean, with glossy golden-brown hair and intelligent eyes. It looked at the Music Teacher and wagged its hairy tail.

The Music Teacher peered closely at it through his glasses. He was perplexed. He was certain that he had never seen the animal before. Perhaps it belonged to the family whose house he was returning from after giving a music lesson to their young daughter.

"Shoo - go away!" he said to the dog, waving his left hand in the direction from which he had come. In his right hand he held a canvas bag containing vegetables that he had purchased in the marketplace, as he usually did when walking home at the end of the day.

The dog sat down on its haunches and looked at him with what appeared to be a great deal of affection.

"GO AWAY!" repeated the Music Teacher, more loudly this time.

The dog stayed where it was. It didn't exhibit the least bit of fear.

The four schoolboys left their spot under the tree and clustered around them.

"This dog doesn't belong to you, uncle?" asked the boy who had called out to him earlier.

"No, I've never seen him before," declared the Music teacher. "I don't know why he's following me."

"Perhaps we can throw stones at it and chase it away," suggested one of the other boys.

"No — please don't do that!" exclaimed the Music Teacher, alarmed. He was by nature a kind person and he had no desire to witness such a beautiful dog come to harm.

He looked around. There was a little shop a short distance away, of the kind that one could see all over town, that sold all manner of sweets and snacks. He pulled out his wallet, extracted a five-rupee note and handed it to the boy who appeared to be the leader of the little gang, saying: "Please go to that shop over there, buy some biscuits, and bring them back here."

The boy took the note and ran off towards the little shop, followed by his three companions. The dog remained where it was, continuing to gaze at the Music Teacher lovingly.

The boys soon returned, with their leader holding a packet of biscuits in his hand.

"Now, throw a few biscuits on the ground at the dog's feet," instructed the Music Teacher. "While it is busy eating them, I am going to slip away. You boys keep feeding the dog while I make my escape."

"Good scheme, uncle! Here, boy! Here are some nice biscuits for you."

The dog turned its attention to the biscuits thrown on at its feet and began to snap them up one by one.

The Music teacher edged away as quietly as he could, then turned around and began to hurry away. He immediately heard a chorus of cries behind him.

"Uncle! It's following you again!"

"It's even left some biscuits on the ground!"

"What a strange dog!"

The Music Teacher turned reluctantly around. There was the dog, right behind, acting for all the world as if it belonged to him.

He felt helpless. Was there no way to get rid of the animal?

The Music Teacher was also a philosopher at heart. He did not know why this particular dog had chosen to bestow its companionship on him to the exclusion of all others, but he decided to accept the situation, at least till he got home. His hope was that he would be able to adroitly maneuver his way to the inside of his bungalow and close the front door firmly in the dog's face. Perhaps it would wander off then.

The schoolboys were looking at him expectantly, their leader still holding the half-empty packet of biscuits in his hand.

"What do you want to do now, uncle?" the boy asked.

The Music Teacher gave a helpless shrug. "You boys can have the rest of the biscuits. I'm going on home, and if the dog wishes to follow me, so be it."

"Very good, uncle, and thanks!" The four young boys happily started dividing up the remaining biscuits among themselves.

The Music Teacher resumed his way homewards, his canine companion now trotting confidently at his side. The dog drew admiring glances from youngsters he passed on the way, with some of them exclaiming: "What a beautiful dog!" and "Can I pet him, uncle?" The Music teacher was tempted to say, "You can even take him home, if you wish," but visions of their parents' reaction prevented him from actually saying so.

After a ten-minute walk, he arrived at the small bungalow that was his home, and paused by the waist-high iron gate that provided entry to the front yard. Could he manage to open the gate just enough to enable him to squeeze through and then close and bolt the gate before the dog could follow him? It was worth a try.

The plan did not work out as he had hoped. As soon as he cautiously opened the gate, the dog darted forward and squeezed through before he could do anything about it. It trotted up the gravel path that led to the front veranda, climbed up the short flight of steps to the veranda, and went and stood by the front door.

The Music Teacher sighed, stepped through the front gate, closed and bolted it behind him, and began to walk towards the front veranda of his house. He stopped as a sudden idea struck him.

What if he were to go around the side of the house to the rear door? Perhaps the dog would stay where it was, by the front door, waiting to be let in.

Accordingly, instead of proceeding straight up the gravel path to the front veranda, he turned to his right and made his way to the side of the house. The dog promptly left its post by the front door, bounded down the veranda steps, and began to follow him.

The Music Teacher's heart sank. He was being outmaneuvered by the animal at every turn!

He made his way around the side of the house, to his rear yard, with the dog following him. Delicious smells were wafting through the open kitchen window that faced the backyard, and he could hear the sound of someone bustling about inside the kitchen. His wife would be in there, preparing their dinner.

He approached the kitchen window, peered through the iron bars, and called out: "My dear!"

His wife, who had her back to him at that moment, gave a convulsive start accompanied by a loud gasp and spun around, her eyes wide with fear. When she saw who it was, her expression of fear gave way to one of considerable annoyance.

"Oh! It's you!" she exclaimed. "What do you mean by creeping up and startling me in this fashion? I thought it was a burglar."

"I am sorry," the Music Teacher said. "But I have a bit of a problem." He quickly explained to her about the dog.

"Ugh!" his wife said. "I am certainly not going to let a filthy animal come into my house! Why can't you shoo it away?"

"Believe me, I've tried," the Music Teacher cried, despairingly. He added, "One thing though — its not some filthy mongrel, it's actually quite a nice looking dog. Take a look."

His wife came up to the window and peered through. The dog looked back at her and wagged its tail enthusiastically.

"H'm — it does looks clean and well-kept," she conceded. "It must belong to someone, it looks too nice and well-fed to be a stray. Can't you find out who it belongs to?"

"Impossible! I wouldn't know where to start," the Music Teacher replied. "I don't even know when and where it started following me. I was alerted to its presence by a group of young schoolboys when I was walking along School Lane, on my way home after going to the marketplace. For all I know, it could have been following me from the marketplace! Perhaps it's owner was shopping there, and it got detached."

"But why would it follow *you*?" his wife demanded.

Her husband shrugged helplessly. "I've no idea why! It's inexplicable. For some strange reason, it's become very attached to me. Why, it wouldn't even be tempted by biscuits." He told her about how he had tried to get the schoolboys to divert the dog's attention. "But now, the important thing is, how am I to get into the house without the dog following me inside?"

His wife was silent for a minute, frowning in thought. Then she said, "I have an idea. I'll come out with a saucer of milk, take it to the back corner of our garden, and set it down there. While I'm doing that, you slip inside, and while its drinking the milk, I'll dash in."

Much to their relief, the plan worked. Now safely inside his house, the Music Teacher collapsed into a chair, and wiped his brow.

"Phew!" he said. "What an experience! I didn't think I would make it inside safely. Now I hope it just goes away."

"It hasn't gone away yet," his wife said. "Look! It's at the window."

Sure enough, the dog was peering at them through the bars of the window that looked out over the rear veranda of the house. Typical of the majority of older houses in this part of the country, the window, like all the other windows of the house, had sturdy iron bars running across its width, to discourage burglars. The space between the bars weren't wide enough for the dog to squeeze through and get inside.

The Music Teacher groaned. "Let's just ignore it, my

dear. I don't know what else to do. Perhaps it will wander off during the night. I can only hope so. I am going to proceed with my usual routine: have my evening bath, say my prayers, and then we'll eat our dinner."

"Shall I give it some food?" asked his wife. "Poor thing – it must be hungry."

Her husband stared at her. "Give it some food? What are you saying? Then it will never go away!"

But while the Music Teacher was having his bath, his wife tossed the dog a couple of *chapatis* through the kitchen window. It eagerly gobbled them up. She also filled a bowl with water, took it to the door that led to the rear veranda, cautiously opened it, placed the bowl of water down on the veranda by the side of the door, and quickly closed the door.

The Music Teacher did not sleep well that night. Images of the dog kept intruding into his dreams. He woke up the next morning feeling tired and out of sorts.

In the mornings, after drinking his coffee, the Music Teacher was in the habit of retiring to a small room in his house, which he called his music room, and sit down cross-legged on a mat on the floor and practice his singing. He was a conscientious man, and he felt that he could teach his students vocal music properly only if he himself practiced every day.

He had seated himself, and was about to begin, when he noticed that his canine companion from the day before was peering at him through the bars of the window.

So it hadn't gone off! He felt frustrated, but forced himself to be calm. He told himself to exclude the dog from his thoughts for the time being and concentrate on practicing his singing as usual. It would be silly to allow this animal to disrupt his daily routine!

He closed his eyes, cleared his throat, and began to practice. But at one point — perhaps the presence of the dog unsettled him, despite his efforts not to let it — he made a grievous error while hitting a note.

Immediately, the dog barked.

The Music Teacher stopped and opened his eyes, astonished. He had never heard this dog bark at him before. But surely, it couldn't have barked because he had made a mistake while singing? That was absurd. It must have seen a bird or squirrel or some such thing outside. But it was sitting on the rear veranda, facing him through the window, not looking at the garden behind it. So it couldn't have noticed a squirrel or bird or anything else in their backyard.

He decided to put it to the test. He resumed his singing, and at one point, deliberately made a mistake.

And immediately, the dog barked at him.

The Music Teacher stopped. This was more than a coincidence. There's another way to clinch this, he thought. He began to sing the same piece from the beginning, being careful not to make any errors.

This time, the dog did not bark, but instead looked at him approvingly and wagged its tail.

The Music Teacher took a deep breath, and continued to practice his singing for an hour, at times making mistakes, whereupon the dog would immediately bark, and at other times, singing perfectly, in which instances the dog would wag its tail and look pleased.

It was incredible! But he felt that there was only one conclusion he could arrive at: strange as it may seem, he was in the presence of a dog that had a ear for vocal music.

At the end of the hour that he normally set aside for his practice, he got to his feet and made his way to the kitchen, where his wife was preparing their breakfast.

He told her what had happened during his singing practice session.

His wife was openly skeptical. "You must have imagined it," she said.

The Music teacher shook his head. "I tested the dog many times, and every time I made an error, it barked."

"But how can a dog be like that?" asked his wife.

"Perhaps it belongs to one of the famous singers who live in our city, and it is accustomed to hearing him sing," said the Music Teacher. "In any case, it appears to be a most unusual dog." He paused, and asked, "Have you given it anything to eat?"

"Look at you!" his wife retorted. "Yesterday, you didn't want me to feed it, for fear that it would never go away."

"Well, now I don't want this dog to leave. I want it to stay."

His wife sighed. "Very well. But only on one condition. I don't want it inside the house. It can live outside."

The Music Teacher thought about it. Where they lived, in the southern part of India, it was warm and humid the year round, except during the monsoon season, when torrential downpours cooled things off considerably. The dog could sleep on the rear covered veranda, he thought, where there was enough shade and breezes to keep it comfortable. They could keep out food and water for it there. Of course, it meant extra work for both of them, taking care of a pet...

His wife was smiling at him, amusedly. They had been married long enough for her to discern what was going through his mind. She said: "Don't worry! I'll keep your four-legged friend well fed and give him plenty of water to drink."

"My dear, you're wonderful," he said humbly, bringing a flush to her cheeks.

The Music Teacher set out for his round of classes that morning with an uplifted heart. His newly acquired canine friend accompanied him to the gate, and stood obediently inside the front yard while he stepped out into the street and closed and bolted the gate.

In the mornings, the Music Teacher's pupils consisted mainly of young housewives whose husbands had gone off to work, and hence had time on their hands that they wanted to put to good use. After his morning round of classes were over, he would usually return home for lunch, followed by a brief siesta before setting out for the afternoon round of classes. His afternoon pupils consisted mainly of girls, ranging in age from the very young to teenagers whose mothers wanted them to learn to sing in the classical, traditional style so as to make them more marriageable when the appropriate time came.

Today, the Music Teacher felt that his morning practice had been more fruitful than usual because of the unusual dog correcting his errors while he practised, and so he taught with a newfound confidence that imparted itself to his pupils.

When he returned home at lunchtime, and back later

in the evening after his afternoon classes, his canine friend came trotting up the gravel path towards the front gate, its tail wagging. After he entered his front yard, it did not try to jump on him, or bump its golden head against his legs, as other large dogs were wont to do; there was a curious dignity and restraint about this dog that appealed to the Music Teacher. He disliked dogs that displayed their affection by jumping on you and almost knocking you down, or ran around your feet, yapping furiously.

I must give the dog a name, he thought. Now, what would be an appropriate name for a dog with a ear for music? He cast his mind back to the names of famous Indian singers who were now deceased. He somehow felt that it would be inappropriate to name the dog after a famous singer who was still alive — what if that singer were to somehow find out that there was a dog named after him? No, that would never do. Then he hit upon the correct name.

"I shall name you Mani," he said to the dog, which was regarding him affectionately. "In honor of that famous singer Madurai Mani Iyer." He went inside and told his wife.

"That is a good name," his wife said. "It will be easy for me to remember."

They got used to having Mani around. They were very pleased that he behaved well and after a while, seemed to grasp that his place was the outside of the house, and he should not attempt to come inside even when they opened the door. The Music Teacher's wife grew quite fond of him. She even took to giving him a regular bath under the garden tap. "It's nice to have Mani to talk to when you're gone teaching your classes," she said. "He seems to understand everything I say!"

"Probably more than me," remarked her husband, drily.

Over the ensuing days and weeks, the Music Teacher felt that his singing had made a huge improvement. This he attributed entirely to his faithful canine companion; by noting when Mani looked disappointed and barked, and when he looked pleased, the Music Teacher gradually took his vocal abilities to new, higher levels. A month later, he was singing and teaching with a gusto and confidence that he had hitherto lacked. His reputation began to spread and he became much in demand, with a proportionate increase in his fees. Due to the increase in his income, he was able to acquire a Vespa scooter that enabled him to zip from one class to the next instead of having to walk or take the city bus.

The winter months were approaching, and with it the beginning of the annual Music Season. This was when daily concerts would be held in various venues around town, showcasing performances by well established singers as well as promising new-comers. To give a performance during the Music Season had long been a dream for the Music Teacher. He now felt confident enough to put his name in. With the help of the parent of one of his students, who was well connected with the Music Academy, his application was approved, and a date and time and venue for his concert was finalized.

For two days prior to the date of his concert, the Music Teacher stayed home and practiced all day in front of his four-legged friend. He lived in a maze of music, scarcely aware of anything else, automatically consuming the meals set before him by his wife.

Finally, the day of the concert arrived. The Music Teacher was slated to give an afternoon performance, at

3:00 pm; the evening slots were reserved for more well-known artists. After a light lunch, he set out for the concert hall with his wife.

The appointed time found him seated on stage, a microphone in front of him, with the violinist who was to accompany his vocal performance seated on his left, and a *tabla* player on his right. He felt both excited and nervous. He could scarcely believe that he was actually realizing his cherished dream of giving a performance at the Music Festival!

Then he looked out over the rows of seats in front of him, and his heart sank. While the first three rows were filled − his wife was seated in the center of the very first row in front, and the remaining seats were filled with his pupils and their parents, plus a few loyal friends who had made the effort to attend − but beyond the first three rows, his eyes beheld rows and rows of empty seats, all the way to the back of the hall. Oddly enough, two well dressed men were seated in the very last row, close to the exit doorway at the rear.

The Music Teacher pulled himself together. Never mind the rows of empty seats, he told himself; after all, he was a relative unknown, so it was only to be expected. He waited for the secretary of the *sabha* to finish his brief introduction, and then launched into his first song.

He sang cautiously at first, then with increasing confidence. As he progressed from one song to the next, the sounds of his vocals flooded the concert hall, sweet and wonderful, causing his audience to applaud enthusiastically at the end of each song.

At the end of his concert, his audience gave him a standing ovation. Waves and waves of applause rolled over him, which he acknowledged, tears of joy running down his cheeks.

As the Music Teacher was making his way off the stage, he saw the two well dressed men who had been seated in the very last row approach him.

"That was a superb performance!" said one.

"Excellent – really excellent!" said the other.

The Music Teacher bowed his head, and murmured: "Thank you, you are too kind."

"Can you spare us a few minutes?" asked the first man. "We would like to talk to you. My name is V.K. Vishwanathan, and this is my friend Harihara Iyer. Perhaps we can go the canteen and talk there. You must be wanting something to drink, your throat must be parched from all that singing."

The idea of having a cup of hot coffee sounded really good to the Music Teacher. "Yes, I will be glad to join you gentlemen in the canteen. But first, I must go and let my wife know of my whereabouts."

"Certainly!" Mr. Vishwanathan said.

The Music Teacher approached his wife, who was still in the concert hall, talking to some of their friends. He quickly told her that two strangers who had attended his concert wished to talk to him, and they were proceeding to the canteen to do so. "You can join us, if you wish," he added. "I am sure that they would have no objection."

His wife demurred. "I think I will head on home," she said. "I would like to get dinner started."

One of their neighbors, who had come to hear his concert and was standing nearby, spoke up. "I will see that she gets home safely, so don't worry. You go ahead and have your meeting."

An hour and a half later, the Music Teacher returned home, with joy in his heart. How pleased and proud his wife would be, when he told her what had transpired in his discussions with Mr. Vishwanathan and his friend. He opened the gate, then paused, with a sense of something being not quite right. Where was Mani, his faithful four-legged friend? He had always come trotting up the moment he heard the sound of the gate being opened.

The Music Teacher hurried up the gravel path towards his little bungalow, calling out: "Mani! Where are you, boy?" He went into his house, where he heard his wife moving around in the kitchen. He went over to the kitchen doorway and asked anxiously, "Where is Mani?"

His wife turned around. Her face was streaked with tears. She shrugged helplessly. "I don't know. When I got home, he was gone. I've looked all over our backyard, everywhere. There's no sign of him."

A cold chill struck the Music Teacher's heart. "But, how could he leave? The only way to leave our compound is via the front gate, and I always keep that closed."

"When I got home, I found the gate to be partly open," his wife said. "When we left the house earlier this afternoon, we must have not latched it properly in our anxiety to get to your concert in time. He must have slipped out and wandered off."

The Music Teacher stood paralyzed for a few moments. Then he cried: "I must go and look for him! Perhaps he has not wandered far."

He hurried out of the house and into the street. For the next hour, he wandered the streets of his neighborhood, anxiously calling out the dog's name.

He was returning home despondently an hour later when, on a little street just couple of blocks away, as he was passing by a small bungalow much like his own, he heard the sound of a young girl's voice, lifted in song. She was singing one of the classical pieces that he was fond of, and in fact had sung at his concert that afternoon.

The Music Teacher came to a halt at the garden gate in front of the house. Seated cross-legged on a mat on the well-lit front veranda was a young girl who could not have been more than ten to twelve years of age. And seated on his haunches in front of her, listening to her sing, was a familiar figure, one that made the Music Teacher's heart leap with joy — his golden-brown canine friend, Mani!

He was about to call out the dog's name when the young girl made a mistake on a note and immediately, Mani barked at her reproachfully, in a manner that was so familiar to the Music Teacher.

The young girl stopped her singing and said, "What is it? Why did you bark?"

Mani just looked at her, tilting his head to one side.

The young girl started to sing again. She sang well on the whole, but once again, made a mistake on a note. The dog barked at once.

"What is it now?" asked the young girl, sounding annoyed. "Why do you bark at certain times? I wish you wouldn't – it disturbs my practice."

"My dear child," called out the Music Teacher cautiously.

The young girl gave a startled exclamation, looked

around and saw the dim figure standing outside the garden gate. She jumped to her feet and dashed into the house through the open front door. A few minutes later, a man who appeared to be in his forties stepped on to the veranda and squinted through the deepening dusk of late evening. "Who are you, sir? Why did you suddenly call out to my daughter?" he asked sharply.

"Please forgive my intrusion," the Music Teacher said. "I was passing by, and I heard your daughter singing, and I stopped. I am a music teacher, you see. Then I spotted my dog —"

The man, who had been staring hard at the Music Teacher meanwhile, interrupted and said: "Sir, you gave a concert this afternoon at the Music Academy, did you not?"

"Yes."

"I was there in the audience. You sang wonderfully! Please do come in." Now looking respectful, the man trotted down to the garden gate, unlatched it, and opened it wide.

"Thank you, but I can only stay for a few minutes," the Music Teacher said, entering the front yard. "Actually, I was out looking for my dog, he had wandered away from my house..." He gestured towards Mani.

"Oh, is that your dog? He suddenly showed up here this afternoon," the man said.

The young girl now stepped out on to the veranda. "Oh, *appa*! Can't I keep him? He's such a nice dog."

"Now, Kamala, if it belongs to this gentleman, you know that we have to give it back."

The Music Teacher said, "Actually, this is a very

unusual dog. He appears to have a ear for music. When someone makes an error in their singing, he will immediately bark."

Young Kamala's eyes grew large and round. "Really, uncle? Is that why he barked while I was practicing just now?"

"Yes, *kondhey*," the Music Teacher replied. "He would do that to me too, whenever I made an error."

Kamala's father looked sceptical.

"I will prove it," the Music Teacher said. "Kamala, please sing, and at some point, make a mistake, on purpose. Can you do that?"

"Yes, uncle." Kamala went over to her mat and sat down on it, cross-legged. She composed herself, closed her eyes, and began to sing. She sang well, and the dog looked on approvingly, wagging his tail. After singing correctly for a few minutes, the young girl faltered on a note.

The dog immediately barked.

"See?" the Music Teacher said. "He will do that every time she makes a mistake."

"My goodness!" Kamala's father said.

"You were praising my singing just now. A great deal of the credit goes to my canine friend," the Music Teacher said. "Having him point out my mistakes when I practiced in front of him improved my singing tremendously."

Kamala said, pleadingly: "Oh, uncle, can't I keep him? Please?"

"Now, now, Kamala, you mustn't ask that," Kamala's father said. "The dog belongs to the Music *vadyar*."

The Music Teacher hesitated. Then he said, "You know, perhaps it is time for Mani — that is the name I gave him, in honor of the famous Carnatic singer Madurai Mani Iyer — to instruct someone else. I think he has taught me enough. Perhaps he himself realized it, which is why he slipped away today. Perhaps it is time that he teaches someone younger." He took a deep breath and said, "I think your daughter should keep the dog."

"Do you mean that, sir?" Kamala's father said. "It is extremely kind of you."

"Thank you, uncle!" cried Kamala. "I will take good care of him."

"Actually, sir, I would be honored if you would give lessons to my daughter," Kamala's father added.

"While I would love to, I fear that I am going to be quite busy, giving more concerts, so my schedule is going to be somewhat erratic. But whenever I have some free time, I will give you a call and see if Kamala would like to have a lesson."

"Thank you very much, sir. Please have some coffee and snacks before you go."

"I am sorry, but I really should return home. I left my house abruptly well over an hour ago to search for Mani, and my wife will be getting worried."

"Very well, sir. Thank you very much for allowing us to keep your musical dog. Please do stop by whenever you wish to see him and us. I plan to attend all your future concerts." Turning to his daughter, Kamala's father said, "*Kondhey*, give the Teacher a *namaskaram* and seek his blessing before he leaves."

Kamala obediently fell to her knees in front of the Music Teacher and bowed down her head. The Music

Teacher was very touched that the father had asked his young daughter to show her respect in this traditional fashion. In these modern times, it is nice to see that there are still people who believe in our old traditions, he thought. He placed his right hand on top of the girl's head and said, "Bless you, my child. I hope you become a famous singer some day."

As he walked home, the Music Teacher felt a tremendous sense of peace. As soon as he entered his house, his wife emerged from their little *puja* room, and said, "I have been praying that you will find Mani. Were you able to?"

The Music Teacher sank into his armchair, and told her what had happened.

"But why did you leave Mani with that girl?" his wife asked. "He's your dog."

The Music Teacher looked at her, quizzically. "But is he really?"

His wife frowned at him. "What do you mean?"

"Remember how he came to be with us? He followed me home. He found *me*, rather than me finding him and bringing him home. So, truthfully, did he really belong to me?"

His wife stared at him, uncertainly. "You are confusing me by saying such things!"

"My dear, have you heard of such a thing as a *muse*?"

"A mouse?" asked his wife, innocently.

The Music Teacher chuckled and said: "No, not a mouse – a *muse*. A muse is a person or personified force who is the source of inspiration for a creative artist. Now, it is important to realize that a muse can take many forms."

"So you are saying that this dog Mani was — what's the word you used — a muse?"

"Yes. He truly helped me. While my singing was good before, he took me to a new level, one that enabled me to give a wonderful concert this afternoon."

The Music Teacher suddenly realized that he had forgotten to tell her about what had transpired after his concert. "My dear, you remember that after the concert, two men wished to speak to me? Their names were Mr. Vishwanathan and Mr. Iyer. It turned out that they are in the business of arranging paying concerts for artists, where people have to buy a ticket to hear the artist perform, and the artist gets paid. They said that they were so impressed with my performance today that they want to arrange paying concerts for me, not only here in town, but in other cities as well. They said they will make all the arrangements, and I would be paid a handsome fee for each concert."

"Why, that is marvelous!" his wife said, her eyes shining. She looked at him proudly. "You will be famous!"

"I hope so. But anyway, isn't it interesting that Mani should choose this day to go and attach himself to someone else? It was as if he *knew* that he had done all he could to help me, that his work with me was done. From what I heard of that little girl's singing, she displays a great deal of promise. He is going to help her, just like he helped me."

His wife nodded, and said, "I understand. Come, go and wash up, and let's have dinner. I have made *payasam* to celebrate your success today."

95

The Jasmine Garden

Ramu was born in a small village deep in southern India, surrounded by green fields of rice and tall coconut palms. His father was a farmer who owned a few acres of land, and earned a modest living growing rice and coconuts on his property, with which he was content.

Ramu's mother, a frail woman, died when he was only six years old. Young children are very resilient, and after a brief period of grief, Ramu quickly rebounded. Moreover, by then he was already enrolled in the district school established by the state government that served their village and other villages in the area, and his school activities kept him busy during the day. His father was busy with his farm, and did not have the time to pay much attention to his son, so young Ramu was left to his own devices. After school, he would spend most of his time swimming in the canal that ran through the village in the company of his playmates, or walking to the nearest town three miles away, where there was more fun to be had. But as he grew older, his father began to ask his help in taking care of his farm, and with chores around the house.

After completing their education at the district school, those students who wished to further their education had to enroll in one of the colleges in town. At that point, Ramu's father, who by then had reached sixty years of age, curtailed his education, deciding that the boy's time would be better spent in helping him farm his land rather than going off to college.

Thus Ramu settled into a quiet rural existence, enlivened only by occasional trips to town whenever his father could spare him. The town, though small, housed a large temple built in ancient times, and he liked going there because there was usually a crowd on most evenings, with a much larger crowd on religious holidays, and Ramu enjoyed the atmosphere of gaiety and excitement. He also liked to stuff himself with delicious, diverse snacks served in the numerous food stalls around the temple perimeter, as this made a welcome change from the simple meals he was accustomed to having at home with his father.

Soon after Ramu turned twenty-five, his father passed away. Ramu was now in full possession of the land his father had so carefully cultivated all his life, and the house he had grown up in, plus some money his father had managed to save up over the years.

Ramu pondered his situation. He wasn't content to just scrape out a meager existence, as his father had, by growing rice and harvesting coconuts. He wanted to put his land to better use. But how?

One evening, when he had gone up to town to attend

a festival being held at the temple that night, it occurred to Ramu that the flower stall located next to the temple entrance was doing a brisk business selling garlands of sweet-smelling jasmine flowers to the throngs of people on their way to the temple.

A sudden idea struck Ramu. He stopped by the flower stall, purchased a garland, and asked the shop owner, "Where do you get your jasmine flowers from?"

"Why, from Kunnathur," the owner replied, naming a village some four miles distant.

"How much do you pay for the flowers?" asked Ramu, nodding towards the rear of the shop, which was filled with heaps of fragrant white jasmine. A thin lady, presumably the shop owner's wife, sat there on a mat, using string and needle to quickly and dexterously create garlands.

The shop owner told him.

Ramu was astonished. He had not known that jasmine flowers could command such a high price.

That night, as he walked home after the temple festivities, Ramu did some serious thinking. Why not convert a part of his land into a jasmine garden? It would require an outlay of some money up front: he would have to drain a few of the shallow rice fields of water, pull out the rice plants, and buy jasmine bushes to plant in their stead. There was the money his father had saved up. Why not put it to good use?

Ramu was not the type to rush into a new scheme rashly. He first consulted some of the older farmers in the village. But they just laughed at him. "You think you can become rich by starting a flower garden? You're just a boy, and you don't understand these things. Don't waste your money. Grow rice and coconuts, like your father and his father before him, and be content with the living it provides."

But Ramu was not one to abandon an idea so easily. He made inquiries in town and found out about a retired teacher whose hobby was to grow the finest jasmine in the garden of his house. He visited this teacher, told him all about himself, and explained his idea about starting a jasmine garden on a portion of his land. The teacher was a kindly man and only too delighted to help.

Over the course of several weeks, the teacher taught Ramu all he knew about growing and taking care of jasmine bushes. He even accompanied Ramu when he went to buy jasmine plants to begin his garden and supervised their planting. Ramu hired two of the friends he had grown up with, who like him had remained in the village, promising to pay them good wages and a share of the profits. "I will grow only the finest jasmine," vowed Ramu.

They all toiled hard together. After six months, with the first flush of spring, Ramu was delighted with his first harvest — they were the finest jasmine flowers he had ever seen.

He and his two worker friends filled big wicker baskets with the results of their labors and took them into town. Ramu was overjoyed when he was able to sell the jasmine at a far better price than he had expected. He rewarded his two faithful friends handsomely

A year later, Ramu was a prosperous flower-grower, surprising the village with his success.

One evening, Ramu was resting on the veranda of his farmhouse with his two friends, exchanging jokes and gossip as they were accustomed to doing after the labors of the day, when they noticed a gray Jeep coming down the dirt lane that led to the house from the paved main road located some fifty yards away. The Jeep pulled up in the open clearing fringed by tall coconut palms in front of the house.

The driver of the Jeep was a stocky man with a powerful build and ferocious moustache, while in the passenger seat next to him sat a prosperous looking individual wearing a spotless white long-sleeve shirt and white dhoti. When the Jeep came to a halt, this individual swung himself off his seat and approached the trio sitting on the veranda, a genial smile on his large face. He appeared to be in his fifties.

"Which one of you is Ramu?" he called out.

"I am Ramu, sir," Ramu said, getting up from his seat.

"Very good!" said the stranger. "I am Vijayan, from Kunnathur village. Are you the Ramu who has the famous jasmine garden?"

Ramu was of a modest disposition and felt awkward to hear his garden described thus. "I have a jasmine garden," he said, humbly.

"I would like to see it, if you don't mind," Mr. Vijayan said.

Ramu was surprised. He stole a quick glance at his friends. They too were staring at the stranger in perplexity.

Vijayan, possibly sensing this, said: "I should probably explain. I, too, am a farmer. I own the largest farm in my village. Many years ago, I converted a portion of my land to a jasmine garden. Then I started hearing about the fabulous jasmine grown by a young man named Ramu, and I was filled with curiosity. So I decided to come and see for myself."

"Very well, sir," Ramu said, descending the veranda steps. "I will be happy to show my garden to you. Please come this way."

Mr. Vijayan took his time touring Ramu's garden. He put forth a number of questions regarding the cultivation and caring of the plants, the cost of maintaining them, and so on, which Ramu readily answered.

Finally, Mr. Vijayan said, "Come, let us go back to your house. There is something important that I would like to discuss with you."

After he had seated his visitor on the veranda in the best chair he had available, Ramu seated himself, and waited expectantly. His two friends had departed while he had been showing Mr. Vijayan around.

Mr. Vijayan cleared his throat and asked, "So, Ramu, you own the jasmine garden and all this land and the house, in entirety?"

"Yes, sir. My father owned it before me, and when he passed away, all of it came to me."

"You have no wife?"

"No, sir. I have not yet married."

"Any brothers or sisters?"

"None, sir. I am an only child."

Ramu's replies appeared to please Mr. Vijayan. He said, "Very good! Now, let me tell you why I came here." He paused, then said, "I would like to buy your jasmine garden."

Ramu was very much taken aback. He had not expected this. His mouth dropped open.

"Buy it, sir?"

"Yes," his visitor replied. Then he added, "Just the jasmine garden. You can still retain ownership of the rest of your land and your house."

Ramu was silent for a few minutes, trying to take in what he had just heard. Then he said, "But why, sir? Why do you wish to buy my garden?"

Vijayan chuckled. "I will be honest with you, my young friend. As I mentioned earlier, I had converted a portion of my land into a jasmine garden. For many years, I had been supplying my flowers to the flower sellers around the temple. Then I started hearing about a young man who had begun to supply flowers that surpassed mine in quality. Naturally, I became curious, so I decided to come and see for myself. Then I decided on the spot that I should expand my jasmine business by buying your garden."

Ramu said, "But sir, my jasmine garden is my livelihood. It is providing me with a good income. Without my garden, what will I do?"

Mr. Vijayan leaned back in his chair and eyed Ramu thoughtfully. After a few moments, he said: "I have heard good things about you, Ramu, so this is what I am prepared to do: after I have completed the purchase, I will hire you at a good salary to take care of the garden and harvest the flowers."

Seeing Ramu hesitate, Vijayan added, persuasively: "You can put the money from the sale of your garden into the bank, and that money will come in useful when you get married and have children. And you will be able to continue to take care of the garden that you have put so much effort into."

Ramu was silent once again. Then he said, "You have made a very good offer, sir. But all this is so sudden.

Could you give me a few days to think it over?"

"Certainly, my boy," Mr. Vijayan said heartily. "I fully understand that you cannot make a big decision like this on the spot. But don't take more than a few days. When I decide on a purchase, I like to see it done quickly." He rose to his feet. "Give me a call in two days."

"But, sir," Ramu said. "I do not have a telephone."

"Oh! Well, no matter. Why don't you come to my house in Kunnathur village, it's only a few miles away. Once you get to my village, you can ask anyone and they will be able to direct you to my house. We can negotiate a price at that time, and also the salary you would like to receive."

Mr. Vijayan stepped off the veranda and walked towards the waiting jeep. He climbed in, and waved goodbye to Ramu. "Remember, come and see me after two days. I will be expecting you."

The jeep drove off. Ramu stared after it, his mind in a whirl.

§

That night, Ramu could barely sleep. He tossed and turned all night, trying to decide what to do. By early morning, he had decided that he had to consult with someone knowledgeable. He immediately thought of the retired teacher who lived in town, who had helped him set up his jasmine garden.

When his two friends arrived later that morning to help him with the garden as usual, Ramu told them about Vijayan's offer. His two friends immediately disagreed on how he ought to proceed.

"Ramu, this garden was your idea, and you toiled hard to produce the finest jasmine possible," his friend Balan said. "Now that you are reaping the rewards of your hard work, this high-and-mighty Vijayan wants to come and take it over. It doesn't seem right — this land belonged to your father, and his father before him."

"But one has to move with the times," the other friend, Sashi, argued. "Ramu will get a nice amount of money from the sale, which he can put in the bank. That money will come in useful when he has a family to support. And he will be allowed to work on the garden at a good salary."

"But he will be working for someone else, not himself," countered Balan. "What's to prevent Vijayan from suddenly saying one day, 'Ramu, I no longer have need of your services. I will operate this garden myself.' Or Vijayan might suddenly reduce his salary at some point, saying that his profits are down, or some such thing. You cannot trust a man like Vijayan."

Ramu looked from one to the other and shook his head. "Neither of you can agree on this — a decision that will change my whole life. That is why I need to consult a third party."

He told them that he intended to go into town and talk to the teacher who had helped him set up the garden. "He is a knowledgeable, honest man and he should be able to guide me well," Ramu said. "You two carry on while I am gone; you know what needs to be done here. I'll try to return as soon as I can."

Ramu set off to the teacher's house in town and was fortunate enough to find him at home. The teacher welcomed him, saying: "Ramu! It is good to see you. It has been a long time. Everything is going well with your jasmine garden, I trust?"

"Actually, sir, it is about my garden that I came to see you," Ramu said. He apprised the teacher of Vijayan's proposal. He ended by asking, "Should I sell my jasmine garden, sir?"

"Quite honestly, Ramu, that is up to you," the teacher replied.

"I was hoping you would be able to guide me, sir. I know you will give me honest advice."

The teacher was touched by the young man's simple faith in him. He said, "Well, in that case, let us analyze the situation and consider the pros and cons of selling versus not selling. First of all, how well acquainted are you with Mr. Vijayan?"

"I don't know him at all, sir; I met him yesterday evening for the first time. But he seemed to be a nice man."

"Oh yes, on the surface he always gives that impression. But underneath, he's a shrewd businessman. Now, did Vijayan mention an actual price he was willing to pay?"

"No, sir. But he said that he would offer me a good price."

"Ah, but do you have an idea of what would be a 'good price' for your jasmine garden?"

"No, sir," replied Ramu honestly. "The land has been in my family for generations, so I have no idea of what it is worth nowadays."

"I can assure you that the price of land around here has gone up significantly over the past ten years," the teacher said. "I would be willing to bet that Vijayan is probably counting on the fact that since the land has been in your family for generations, and you have been so busy developing and growing your jasmine, you are probably unaware of what your land is truly worth. Also, you have to remember, Ramu, that it is not just the land that you are selling. Situated on it is a prosperous business, the jasmine garden. Do you know how much in profit you made from your garden in the past year? Even a rough figure would do."

Ramu told him.

The teacher uttered a low whistle and looked impressed. "That much? You can be sure that Vijayan would have taken that into account. Now, Ramu, the reality is that Vijayan's 'good price' will be substantially below what your jasmine garden is truly worth. That is how he operates."

Ramu was silent. The teacher had raised points that had not occurred to him. He felt very glad that he had decided to consult him.

"There is another thing that you need to know, sir. Vijayan has promised to hire me at what he said would be a 'good' salary to take care of the jasmine garden for him."

"I see. But as you just informed me, you are making a very good profit from your garden, Ramu. Logically, Vijayan will not pay you as much in salary as you make in profits, because he needs to make a profit for himself."

"That is very true, sir," Ramu said.

"Vijayan's promise to hire you to continue to work on your garden, which at first glance sounds like he's doing you a big favor, has no doubt been made because it is convenient for him to have you on the spot, taking care of the jasmine plants. He's probably made inquiries and discovered that you know how to produce the finest jasmine flowers in the district."

The teacher paused and looked at Ramu keenly. "Now, having heard all this, do you still want to sell your jasmine garden to Vijayan?"

"No, sir, I do not," Ramu said, determinedly. "This morning, I wasn't so sure, but the more I have understood how Vijayan operates, the more I feel that I should not sell to him. The land has been in my family for generations. I have worked hard to make my flower garden a success, and now that I am reaping the rewards, Vijayan wants to take it away from me, probably at a price well below what it's truly worth."

"I agree wholeheartedly with your sentiments, Ramu." The teacher's face then became grave. "But there's another point you have to consider. It is rather unpleasant, I'm afraid, but I would be remiss if I did not mention it to you. This Vijayan has developed a reputation for getting what he wants, by any means." He paused and gave Ramu a significant look.

Ramu asked, "Are you trying to say, sir, that he will force me to sell my jasmine garden to him?"

"He cannot force you by legal means, but on the other hand, he might use some other methods to make you sell."

Ramu stared at the teacher. "What other methods, sir?"

The teacher looked distinctly uneasy. "This is all just hearsay, mind you, but I have heard of instances where some farmers who had refused to sell to Vijayan had their crops damaged in the middle of the night very mysteriously, things like that. Vijayan can be pretty ruthless, is what I've heard."

A cold chill went up Ramu's spine. The last thing he wanted was to have his beloved jasmine bushes hurt in any way. Then a thought occurred to him. "But didn't those farmers go to the police?"

The teacher said sadly, "It's rumored that our local police station chief is in Vijayan's pocket. That is, Vijayan pays him off handsomely whenever there's a spot of trouble, and the police never take any action against him."

"But that's terrible!" cried Ramu.

"Yes, I know, but what can one do? That is the reality in many of our rural districts. But come to think of it," added the teacher, thoughtfully, "I've heard that this sort of thing is common in big cities as well, where criminal gangs operate with impunity because they've paid the police off."

A sense of despair settled upon Ramu. "Is there nothing I can do, sir?"

The teacher looked at the troubled young man, and a wave of sympathy washed over him. Ramu embodied the kind of simple, honest, hardworking young farmer who formed the backbone of the country, he thought. He said, "It's possible that I may be able to help you –"

"Do you mean that, sir?" Ramu said, hope dawning on his face.

"Well, I can't promise you results, but there's a good friend of mine who might be able to offer assistance. I have never asked him for favors before, but this is a good cause, and I think he will be interested. Perhaps it is time that Mr. Vijayan was taught a lesson, that he cannot do whatever he wishes to in this district. You said that Vijayan has given you two days in which to provide your answer, correct?"

"Yes, sir."

"I will give my friend a call today. Why don't you

come back tomorrow, and I will let you know."

§

Two days later, Ramu presented himself at Mr. Vijayan's large house. He was feeling extremely nervous, but he steeled himself to the task in front of him.

Vijayan welcomed him in his usual hearty manner. "Ah, Ramu – right on schedule! Very good. Let us sit at this table. This is my lawyer, Mr. Sabu. He has drawn up all the necessary documents. He will fill in the price and your salary and other terms after we have negotiated."

Mr. Sabu, a thin cadaverous looking gentleman wearing severe looking spectacles, nodded at Ramu and resumed his review of the sheaf of documents on the table in front of him.

"But first, something to drink," said Vijayan. "You must be thirsty from the walk from your village." He called out, "Namboodiri! Three coffees please, quickly!"

Three steaming tumblers of coffee soon arrived. Vijayan took an appreciative gulp, smacked his lips, and said, "Excellent! Now, let's discuss the price for your jasmine garden and so forth."

Ramu drank half his coffee to slake the dryness in his mouth. He took a deep breath, and said, "Actually, sir, I came to tell you that I have decided not to sell."

There was a silence. Vijayan stared at Ramu, the genial smile wiped off his face as with a sponge. The lawyer, Sabu, was also staring at him through his glasses.

Ramu felt like he might faint from the tension that was now palpable in the room. He licked his lips, and said, "I am very sorry sir, but the land has been in my family for generations. Also, I put in a great deal of effort to develop my jasmine garden. So I do not wish to sell."

Vijayan leaned back in his chair. "Are you sure, Ramu? I am prepared to make you a good offer."

"Yes, sir, I am quite sure."

Now Vijayan looked faintly menacing. "You are making a big mistake, Ramu."

Ramu stayed silent, his head bowed, staring at the polished surface of the table. His heart was hammering in his chest. Would Vijayan try to do him harm right then and there? Surely he wouldn't do that, would he?

Much to Ramu's relief, Vijayan leaned back in his chair and sighed. "Well, if that is your decision, so be it. I just hope nothing happens to that precious garden of yours."

Ramu looked up, his stomach tightening with fear. "What do you mean, sir?"

Vijayan was deliberately vague. "Accidents happen, you know. There are vandals that roam around this district. I hope they don't take it in their heads to harm your beautiful jasmine plants."

Ramu felt shaky, but forced himself to stand up. "Thank you, sir, for considering an offer for my property. I hope you understand why I do not wish to sell. I hope there are no hard feelings."

"That's the nature of business," Vijayan said, showing his teeth in a mirthless smile. He looked like a shark that has been deprived of its victim. "Not everyone I approach wants to negotiate a transaction at first. But it is surprising how most of them change their mind subsequently," he added, with a grim chuckle. "If you ever change your mind, don't hesitate to come back. Mind you, I may not offer you the same generous price that I had in mind today."

As Ramu walked back to his home, he was assailed by doubts. Had he done the right thing? Vijayan's menacing words kept running through his head. He almost turned around to retrace his steps back to the man's house, to tell him that he had changed his mind. Then he told himself, I must be brave. I cannot let my friend, the teacher, down. He's done so much to try and help me, so I must see this through.

§

It was past midnight on that same night. A full moon cast its soft, misty-white glow over the countryside, resulting in a world of alternating pale light and shadows. Silence hung over Ramu's farm, broken only by the occasional faint rustling sound of nocturnal creatures going about their business in the bushes and trees.

Two shadowy figures stealthily entered Ramu's jasmine garden. The moonlight glinted off the gleaming, wicked looking scythe each one held in his right hand. They approached one of the jasmine bushes, and began to viciously hack off the branches. Before long, the bush lay completely destroyed.

Just then, beams of powerful light sprang up, pinning the two men in their glare. A steely voice yelled: "This is the police! Stop where you are! If you try to run away, you will be shot!"

The two men immediately froze, staring wild-eyed in the direction of the powerful lights.

The same steely voice yelled out, "Drop those scythes

and raise your hands!"

The intruders did as they were told. They saw, advancing towards them out of the darkness, a tall, lean man dressed in the uniform of a Police Inspector, flanked by two constables. All three of them carried powerful torches, and the Inspector had his gun drawn and was pointing it at the two men with a very steady hand.

Meanwhile, Ramu was standing anxiously on the edge of the veranda of his house. He could hear the Police Inspector's shouted commands from the direction of his beloved jasmine garden. After what seemed to him like an eternity, but was in reality only about five minutes or so, he saw torch beams making their way through the coconut palms that surrounded his house. He quickly stepped to the back of the veranda and switched on the veranda light.

The Police Inspector and the two constables, each one holding a handcuffed man in a tight grip, arrived at the clearing in front of the veranda. Ramu immediately recognized one of the handcuffed men.

"Inspector, that man—" he pointed at the swarthy individual "—is Mr. Vijayan's driver!"

"Is he, indeed?" responded the Inspector. "Well, let us hear what he has to say about his presence in your garden in the middle of the night, destroying your jasmine plants."

"Did they destroy many of the plants?" inquired Ramu anxiously.

"Just one. I let them hack one down so that I could obtain clear evidence of their intentions, for the judge."

"Inspector Anand, I cannot thank you enough for coming down all the way from Trivandrum to look into this matter," Ramu said, gratefully.

"Don't give it a second thought," said the Police Inspector. "When my teacher friend explained the situation, I was only too glad to come down. People like Vijayan have to be taught a lesson." He smiled reassuringly at Ramu and added, "We're going to take off now. First, I am going to stop by Mr. Vijayan's house and ask him to explain why his driver was trying to wreck your jasmine garden in the middle of the night. I'm sure he will deny all knowledge of the matter, but it will at least put a scare in him."

Ramu watched the departing police jeep with relief in his heart.

Next morning, he got up at his usual time, and was working in his garden, clearing up the twigs and branches of the destroyed jasmine bush, when his two friends, Balan and Sashi, arrived. They gaped at the sight of the wreckage.

"Ramu! What happened here?"

Ramu filled them in on the events of the previous night.

Balan's face lit up and he danced a little jig. "Aha!" he cried. "Vijayan's wings have been clipped! Hooray!"

But Sashi was shaking his head, mournfully. Balan stopped jumping around and glared at him. "Why aren't you rejoicing?" he demanded.

"Do you think a setback like this will stop Vijayan?" Sashi asked.

"You're talking nonsense!" retorted Balan. "Vijayan's own driver was caught red-handed."

"Vijayan will find a way to squirm out of it. He has money and influence. He will lie low for a while, and then resume his attacks, mark my words. Vijayan has lost face in this episode, and he will want revenge."

Ramu stared at him, his anxiety returning. "Do you mean that, Sashi?"

"If Vijayan tries any more of his dirty tricks, Ramu will just contact his friend the Police Inspector in Trivandrum!" Balan said.

"How often do you think that Police Inspector will come dashing down to help?" persisted Sashi. "I am sure he had plenty of crimes to attend to back there!"

Ramu uttered a hollow groan and sat down on the ground, covering his face with his hands.

§

It was five years later. At a busy street corner in the city of Trivandrum stood a little shop that sold a variety of cold drinks and all manner of sweets and snacks. It was a popular place in the neighborhood and did a brisk business.

A customer stopped by and called out: "Ramu! One ice-cold Coca-Cola, please, to cope with this heat."

More customers stopped by. After that, there was a temporary lull in business, and Ramu sat down on his stool and gave himself up to reflection.

As his friend Sashi had prophesied, Vijayan managed to wiggle out of the charges brought against him. After lying low for about a year, he began to put the word out about his displeasure with Ramu, and to make fearsome threats about what he was going to do to him.

By that time, Ramu had got married, to the pretty daughter of a widow who lived in his village. When he heard about Vijayan's threats, he grew fearful not only for his own safety but also the safety of his young wife. As Sashi had said, how often could he ask the Police Inspector from Trivandrum to come down and protect him?

After some thought, and after consulting with his friend and mentor the teacher once again, Ramu reluctantly came to the conclusion that the the best thing would be to leave the area. He considered having his two good friends take care of his property, but upon reflection, realized that Vijayan would be able to destroy his beloved jasmine plants — he could not reasonably expect his friends to guard the garden night after night. So he actively sought a buyer for his entire farm. With the teacher's help, he had been fortunate to find a buyer who offered him a good price. With the money from the sale, he moved to Trivandrum with his young wife, and set up the little shop. The shop was close to Inspector Anand's residence. He felt safe from Vijayan here; he felt that the latter would not dare pursue him to Inspector Anand's territory.

The shop did a good business, and he was making far more money than he had ever done with his jasmine garden. But Ramu grew wistful whenever he recalled the simple, happy life he had led in his village. Perhaps someday Vijayan would get arrested for some other transgression, unable to bribe his way out of the charges brought against him, thought Ramu. I could then sell this shop at a good price and move back to my village. That thought cheered him.

He was interrupted in his reverie by a bright-eyed little girl who had been playing with her dolls in the interior of the shop. She came up to him and tugged at his *dhoti.* He hoisted her into his lap and gave a her a fond hug.

"*Achan* (father), I like it when you bring me here," the little girl said. "I like your shop."

"Ah, my child, but you should have seen the jasmine garden I owned," Ramu replied. "I grew the finest jasmine in the district…"

A Nation's Call

The year was 1942, and a great wave of national emotion was sweeping over India, as the voice of a diminutive leader named Gandhi called to the nation's millions to arise and strive to achieve India's independence from British rule via peaceful demonstrations and non-violent resistance. Gandhi's call touched the hearts and minds of the rich and poor, male and female, young and old, and they responded to the noble call for freedom, laying aside their daily lives to give their all for the country's cause.

But in a modest two-storey house on a narrow street in the southern city of Madras, the attention of a middle aged couple was focused on matters much closer to home. It was nine o'clock at night and a steady drizzle was falling outside, and the only sound to break the stillness of the street was the monotonous sound of dripping water. The middle aged couple, seated in their living room, were engaged in an intense discussion. The husband was one Mr. Raghunath, a plump gentleman of medium height, who with perseverance, hard work, and a rare capacity for pleasing a succession of British and Indian bosses, had over the past thirty years risen from the position of a clerk to Department Head of a prominent government agency.

"Our son is being an obstinate fool," he was saying, frowning in annoyance. "He has been turning down all the marriage proposals that have come our way over the past year. He even had the audacity to refuse to consider an excellent alliance, the daughter of Judge Neelakantan. They are a very distinguished family. And prior to that, when that wealthy businessman offered his daughter, along with a handsome dowry, our son again refused. I tell you, I am getting quite fed up with his attitude!"

His wife Ganga, though in agreement with her husband's feelings about their son's steadfast refusals, tried to soothe her husband. "There is no use getting angry over it," she said. "It is our ill-luck, that he is not like other dutiful sons who listen to their parents when it comes to something as important as marriage. He says he wants to concentrate on using his legal skills to serve the nation."

"At least he studied hard and obtained his Bachelor of Law degree," conceded Mr. Raghunath. "But he should get married before he becomes too old. Once past a certain age, his chances of finding a suitable girl will be greatly diminished. All our relatives, and our neighbors, and even my colleagues at work, are constantly asking me why he is still unmarried."

"Then why don't you fix up a suitable match without asking him?" suggested his wife. "There is no use asking boys about these things – they do not know what is good for them. Were we consulted before we were married? No, our parents fixed it up and we could not do anything but go through the ceremony. Now, if you find a good girl for Vijay and make all the arrangements, he will find it impossible to back out."

"Perhaps you are right," responded her husband. "I actually have a good alliance in view. You know my old classmate Samban? He is now a prominent lawyer with two daughters. The older one has been married off, and he is looking for a suitable groom for the younger girl. He called me last week asking if I would be interested in having her marry Vijay. It would be a very good match. Since Samban is a well known lawyer, he will be of tremendous help to further our son's law career."

"I have heard of him," said Ganga. "But they say the girl is not pretty."

"That's all nonsense!" Mr. Raghunath retorted angrily. "Who says she isn't pretty? Besides, what does it matter? It is not like our son is all that handsome."

"Oh, but he is," responded his wife loyally. "What about her horoscope?"

"You know that I don't care much about that sort of thing," said her husband. "Astrologers and horoscopes are not infallible. This is a good alliance, and there is no use entertaining unnecessary doubts and fears."

His wife looked dubious. She was a very religious lady and believed firmly in old customs and traditions. "I still think..." she began.

"No!" Mr. Raghunath interrupted, firmly. "I am going to telephone Samban forthwith, telling him that we would very much like to see Vijay get married to his daughter, and asking him to proceed with setting up the engagement ceremony as soon as possible."

While this conversation was going on between the parents, the object of their discussion, their son Vijay, was in his bedroom upstairs, and he could not help but overhear every word. He had told his parents earlier that he was going out after dinner to meet some friends, but had later changed his mind because of the rain. His parents were unaware that he was still in the house and hence had not bothered to lower their voices, so Vijay had heard their entire discussion.

Vijay was an intelligent young man with a flair for debate. He had joined his college's Debating Society where his oratorical skills had garnered him a succession of prizes, and he had represented his college in debating competitions with other colleges in town. However, his father severely disapproved of these kinds of activities, which he felt came in the way of his studies. He wanted his son to focus only on his college courses and earn top marks in his examinations. He did not like Vijay to read anything other than his textbooks. If he saw his son with a magazine or some other reading material not connected with his courses, he would sharply reprimand him. Sometimes even his mother would join in. Vijay tried to bear it all with resignation and fortitude.

Vijay's most ardent desire was to play a significant role in India's struggle for freedom from British rule. He felt that life otherwise would be most unworthy. He was even prepared to give up his career for such a noble cause. But his father called them 'wild dreams' and 'the childish fancies of an immature person'. So Vijay took to keeping his activities and participation in freedom marches and rallies a secret from his parents.

Vijay's ideals were what had led to his refusals to get married. He felt that once he yielded to the traditional 'arranged marriage', he would be sacrificing his mission in life and reducing himself to the traditional role of a dutiful husband, working and earning for his family. He imagined what his daily life would be after marriage: get up early in the morning, have his bath, eat breakfast, go off to work, return in the evening, talk about the events of the day, have dinner, perhaps read a bit after that, then off to bed. In all probability his parents would induce him to continue living in their house, as was traditional. He could imagine his father saying: "Why do you want to squander a good part of your salary in having a place of your own? There is enough room in this house for both you and your wife; moreover, she will be good company for your mother. She can help your mother with cooking and other household chores."

If, after marriage, he wished to play a part in India's fight for freedom, Vijay imagined that his wife (unless she was a uniquely understanding person) would probably join his parents in remonstrating: "Why do you want to risk your job and waste your time on such things? Let us sit together in the evenings, like one happy family." He knew that he would be unhappy in such a role, and he shrank from imposing his unhappiness on some poor girl who would be chosen as his bride.

These thoughts tormented Vijay often. He could not

reconcile himself to his parents' conventional ideas, just as they were unable to comprehend his idealistic outlook.

The conversation that Vijay overheard that night, culminating in his father's decision to push ahead with an arranged marriage for him, brought renewed anguish to his heart. He laid awake in bed all night long, unable to sleep. What was he to do? Should he shatter his ideals as impractical fantasies and submit to the inevitable? No doubt that would make his parents happy. But had he not a duty to answer his nation's call?

A glance at the clock on his bedside table told Vijay that it was only 4:30 am. There was still over an hour to go before sunrise, and it was all dark and quiet outside. He slipped out of bed, got dressed and slipped out of the house. The rain of the previous night had ceased and the air felt damp and cool. He decided that he would walk to the beach, which was located only half a mile away. A walk along the seashore might help to clear his mind.

Arriving at the beach, Vijay took his sandals off and walked barefoot on the sand. The fine grains felt soft and warm under his feet. He walked to the seashore, where the sand was still damp from the retreating tide. The rhythmic sound of the waves advancing to the shore and then retreating, following their timeless pattern, brought some solace to his mind. The eastern skyline was beginning to lighten, heralding the dawn of a new day. At that early hour, the beach was mostly deserted, with only a few early risers strolling along the seashore. He selected a clean spot, sat down and gave himself up to thought.

To Vijay it seemed like there was only one way out of the difficulty, and that was to remove himself from his parent's house and strike out his own path. He felt that to live any longer under that roof would cost him his very soul. Painful though it might be for his parents, he had to leave. But his departure would have to be done in secret; he could not bear the thought of the painful scene which would undoubtedly occur, with his father shouting and yelling, and his mother crying, if he were to tell them of his decision.

Vijay watched the sun peep up over the horizon, sending its shimmering rays over the placid ocean, and bestowing a golden path from the shore to the horizon. With the sunrise, he felt that the struggles in his mind had been replaced with calmness and a tremendous resolution. He got up to go home, feeling like a new man.

When he arrived home, he found his father in the front garden, inspecting the rose bushes and other plants that their gardener, acting on his instructions, had planted over the years. He looked up as Vijay opened the gate that provided entry to the front yard of the house from the street outside.

"You're up early today," his father remarked.

"I woke up early and decided to take a walk to the beach," Vijay said. "It was very peaceful there at this time of day."

"Very good."

A determined expression came into Mr. Raghunath's face. He cleared his throat, and said, "Vijay, I want you to be available on Wednesday evening. Your mother and I are going to visit my friend Samban, and I want you to accompany us."

Based on the conversation between his parents that he had overheard the previous night, Vijay could well guess why. This visit would be so that the prospective bride and groom could meet each other, and the preliminary details of the wedding be hashed out. Knowing his father, Vijay thought it likely that he would have told his friend Samban to arrange for the traditional engagement ceremony to take place right then and there.

"Very well, father," said Vijay meekly.

His father looked astonished. He had fully expected some resistance on Vijay's part, and had been prepared to do battle. Vijay's ready acquiescence took him aback. Recovering himself, he said: "Excellent! Well, that's settled, then."

Vijay spent the greater part of that day in his bedroom with the door closed, telling his parents that he had some important law files to go over. He filled up a large suitcase with as much of his clothes and books as would fit in there. When he came downstairs to join his parents for meals, he went out of his way to be nice to them, listening quietly when they brought up the issue of marriage. His parents were pleasantly surprised at this change in their son's demeanour, and began to entertain hopes that he was now veering around to their point of view.

Early next morning, Mr. Raghunath was sitting on the front veranda, drinking his morning coffee and reading the newspaper, as was his usual custom, when he heard his wife's voice raised in a shriek of dismay from the interior of the house. Startled, he rose hurriedly to his feet and rushed inside, to see his wife collapsed on one of the chairs of their dining table, sobbing.

"What is the matter?" gasped Mr. Raghunath.

She thrust a sheet of notepaper at him. Mr. Raghunath grabbed it from her hand, and read the note, written in his son's precise, neat handwriting:

Dear mother and father:

I know that what I am about to tell you will upset you greatly, and you might even curse me as an unfilial son. I have decided to go away and strike my own path. It is only after the deepest deliberation that I have taken this action. For a long time, I have felt that there is a duty to my country that is higher than the duty towards my parents. I have realized that my conscience can only be satisfied by joining the struggle for our nation's independence from under the yoke of our British rulers. But for some time, I have realized that you do not truly understand my mission, and you entertain quite different ideas of my duties in life. It was with the deepest pain that I overheard your decision to fix up my marriage without my consent. The day of my engagement ceremony is fast approaching, and I felt that I should act before that date, so as not to cause pain to the bride and her family as well.

I have but one request. Please do not try to locate my whereabouts and come after me. I need to pursue my actions with complete freedom.

Perhaps some day you will find it in your heart to forgive me for this action I have taken.

Your loving son,

Vijay

If a thousand thunderbolts had fallen on their heads, the shock could not have been greater for Vijay's parents. They had never expected this of him, especially at this juncture, when they were about to fix him up in matrimony. Mr. Raghunath, predictably, lost his temper and cursed his son for the dishonor he had brought to his family by his disappearance literally just days before the engagement ceremony. What would he tell his friend Samban? What would his relatives, neighbors and colleagues say?

Meanwhile, Vijay's mother was nearly prostrate with grief at the loss of her only son. She began to reproach herself for attempting to get Vijay married against his wishes, and cursed herself for the part that she had played in it.

§

Five years had passed since Vijay had left his parents' house. During these five years, Mr. Raghunath and his wife had not laid eyes on their son, or heard from him. They had given up all hope of ever seeing him again.

It was the night of August 14, 1947. Mr. Raghunath and his wife stayed up late to listen to the radio broadcast of India's first Prime Minister, Jawaharlal Nehru, announcing the country's freedom from British rule:

"Long years ago, we made a tryst with destiny; and now the time comes when we shall redeem our pledge, not wholly or in full measure, but very substantially. At the stroke of the midnight hour, when the world sleeps, India will awake to life and freedom.

A moment comes, which comes but rarely in history, when we step out from the old to the new — when an age ends, and when the soul of a nation, long suppressed, finds utterance. It is fitting that at this solemn moment we take the pledge of dedication to the service of India, and her people, and to the still larger cause of humanity…"

The speech had gone on for another nine minutes. After it ended, Mr. Raghunath switched the radio off, leaned back in his chair, and sat staring at the radio with unseeing eyes, his thoughts far away. His wife, too was silent, her eyes filling with tears.

"Vijay's dream has been realized," she whispered.

Mr. Raghunath stayed silent. Then he got up tiredly and made his way upstairs to their bedroom, his wife following him.

The following morning Mr. Raghunath woke up later than usual. He made his way to his front veranda, where he sat reading the newspaper and drinking his coffee, following his typical morning routine. He heard the sound of many distant voices, shouting *"Jai Hind!"*, coming closer. Must be one of those processions to mark India's first day as a free country, he thought.

He was somewhat surprised to see the procession turn into his narrow street. At the head of the procession was a slowly moving old convertible car with its top down. Sitting in the rear seat was a lean figure with long hair and a luxuriant beard, with a garland of marigold flowers around his neck. He was dressed in the saffron-colored robes of a *sanyasi* — a holy man. Behind the car walked a long procession of men, women, and children, enthusiastically waving the Indian flag and shouting *"Jai Hind!"* and *"Bharat Mata ki Jai!"*.

Mr. Raghunath watched them idly as they came up the narrow street. He fully expected the procession to pass on by his house, and was astonished when the car came to a halt in front of his garden gate.

One of the men at the head of the procession stepped forward, opened the car door, and helped the Swami ji out. The holy man stood for a moment, using a cane for support, gazing at the house with a faint smile upon his lips. Then he walked towards the front gate, which one of his followers unlatched. The Swami ji walked slowly up the gravel path towards the front veranda, his eyes fixed kindly on Mr. Raghunath, while the crowd streamed into the compound.

Mr. Raghunath was thoroughly bewildered by this time. Why had this holy man chosen to come to his house? He hurriedly scrambled up from his chair and brought the palms of his hands together in a polite *namaste*, while bowing his head as a sign of respect. Meanwhile, his wife Ganga, attracted by the noise of the procession, had emerged from the house and stood on the veranda just outside the front door, staring in wonder at the crowd and at the thin bearded figure of the holy man, swathed in a saffron robe, coming towards them.

The Swami ji climbed the short flight of steps that led up to the veranda, with one of his followers assisting him, and stood before Mr. Raghunath and his wife.

He eyed them fondly and said in a gentle voice, "My dear parents, don't you recognize me?"

Ganga was the first to recover from the shock. With a scream, she rushed forward and hugged the thin figure, crying: "Vijay? Our Vijay? Is it possible? Oh, my son, my beloved son, you have come back at last, after all these years!" She broke down and sobbed, smiling through her tears. Mr. Raghunath, who had been stricken dumb, recovered and with a wave of joy sweeping over him, came forward and embraced his son. The crowd cheered and clapped, and cries of "*Jai*, Swami Vijay!" filled the air.

Vijay, after embracing his parents, turned to the crowd and raised his hand for silence. Once the crowd had quieted down, he said: "My dear friends, you have done me a tremendous service by bringing me to my parent's house, the home where I grew up, on this glorious day, which our beloved country celebrates as a truly free nation. Now I have but one request: please allow me to spend a few days alone with my dear parents, whom I have not seen in five years. We have much to say to each other."

"We will do as you wish, Swami ji," came the response, and with cries of "*Jai Hind!*" the crowd began to disperse.

Vijay turned to his parents and said, "Come, mother and father, let us go inside and sit and talk." Using his cane for support, he walked into the house and sank into a chair.

"Vijay!" cried his mother. "You look so thin and tired! What has happened to you?"

Vijay smiled at her. "There is much that I have to tell you both. Mother, may I trouble you for a glass of water? Or fruit juice, if you have any?"

Ganga dashed off to the kitchen, and returned a few minutes later, carrying a glass of orange juice and a plate containing *murukkus* and a sweet.

Vijay drank the juice, leaned back in his chair, and began:

"My dear parents, let me begin at the point when I disappeared from your lives five years ago. I set forth by train for Mahatma Gandhi's ashram in Sabarmati, Gujarat, arriving there some four days later. Like for many others, he became my spiritual leader and guide. I took an active

129

part in numerous demonstrations against the British. In many of these protest rallies, although we marched peacefully, carrying no weapons of any kind, we were charged and beaten severely with *lathi* sticks by policemen headed up by British officers. I sustained numerous broken bones and other wounds many times, but as soon as I healed, I would rejoin the glorious fight for India's freedom. Although the British could hurt our bodies, they could not quell our spirit. Eventually, I was arrested and thrown in prison, along with many of our other Freedom Fighters, including Gandhi ji himself.

During this time, I found myself becoming more and more spiritual. During my sojourn in prison, I read our ancient texts: the *Vedas*, the *Upanishads*, the *Baghavad Gita*, and so on, and began to convey their deep messages to others. I took on the life of a *sanyasi* and found great joy in showing others the path to a more spiritual life.

During my entire absence, I never forgot you, my dear parents. But because of my activities as a freedom fighter I did not try to contact you. I did not want the British to come and trouble you, and father, I did not want you to lose your good job because of my activities. Therefore I endeavored to keep our relationship a secret.

Finally, the glorious day arrived when all of our hard work bore fruit and our beloved country was granted independence. I decided that my first act in a free India would be to come and see you, my parents, and beg your forgiveness for the abrupt manner in which I left you five years ago."

Vijay paused and a look of deep sadness passed over his face. "Now, I wish to tell you another thing about me, and I want you to be strong."

"What is it, my son?" his mother asked, with considerable anxiety.

"I have been diagnosed with cancer, and it has advanced to the point where doctors have given their considered opinion that I have but six months to live."

His parents stared at him, frozen in shock. Then his mother collapsed, weeping like her heart would break. Tears welled up in Mr. Raghunath's eyes and ran down his cheeks. He leaned forward and grasped his son's hand.

"Please be strong for me, dear parents. I have decided that I want to spend the last six months of my life in this house, the house I grew up in, in the company of the two people whom I love the most in this world."

Over the next few months, Mr. Raghunath's house was besieged by a stream of anxious visitors, who came to inquire about Swami Vijay's health. Letters poured in from all over the country. Mr. Raghunath's heart filled with pride at seeing how famous his son had become, but those sentiments were mixed with anguish as he witnessed his son's inexorable decline week after week. He sent for the best doctors in town, but all medical aid proved futile and now it was only a question of time.

Suppressing his grief, Mr. Raghunath kept near his son every day. A complete transformation had come over him. He was no longer the strict father of prior years who had attempted to dictate the course of his son's future with no consideration for his feelings and desires. They sat together on the veranda and conversed like they never had before. Vijay sketched out his vision and ideas for the future of India. Mr. Raghunath began to realize − rather late, perhaps − that his son was a brilliant visionary with a strong sense of morals.

Some six months after his arrival, the doctor who came to check on Vijay every week took Mr. Raghunath aside and informed him that the end was near. Vijay by then had become so weak that he was bedridden. He had made his intentions clear that he did not wish to go to a hospital and preferred to pass away at home.

One evening, he summoned his parents and whispered to them: "My dear mother and father, I have a feeling that I will not survive the night. Please do not grieve unduly — I have achieved my life's dream of fighting for a free India and have been fortunate enough to witness my country's emergence as an independent nation. I could not have asked for more."

Mr. Raghunath could not restrain his tears and said: "My beloved son, please forgive me for being the hard-hearted selfish fool that I was once. You have opened my eyes and liberated my soul. With the money I have saved up, I am going to establish an *ashram* in your name, and I will henceforth devote the rest of my life to furthering your vision for our beloved country's future."

Tears filled Vijay's eyes and he smiled happily. Then his eyes closed for one last time, while his parents knelt by his bedside and prayed.

Partition

(The story that follows this preface is based largely on true events. On the 15th of August 1947, India was granted freedom from British rule, but simultaneously, what had been for thousands of years one nation, India, was partitioned into two separate countries: India and Pakistan. The partition took place due to the unrelenting efforts of a handful of Muslim leaders, who campaigned hard for the creation of a separate country that would be the new homeland for the tens of millions of Muslims scattered throughout India. And although Mahatma Gandhi and a few other leaders were against splitting up the nation in this fashion, they were overruled.

The partition set in motion one of the largest mass migrations of the 20th century. It is estimated that over 10 million people crossed the borders between the two countries in 1947 - 48, as millions of Muslims living in India decided to move to their new homeland, Pakistan, while millions of Hindus who suddenly found themselves living in what was now Pakistan fled to India.

Unfortunately, the partition set off sectarian violence in both countries. The level of horrific bloodshed that followed was totally unforeseen by the British and the leaders of the two countries. Estimates say that anywhere between one to two million men, women and children were massacred.)

Around 9:30 am on a cool autumn morning, a taxi drew up outside a prosperous looking two-story house on a quiet street in Amritsar, India. A young man with a shoulder bag stepped out and paid off the driver. He approached the iron gate that bisected the high walls that surrounded the bungalow's compound, and hailed the white-haired old man sitting on the front veranda.

"Mr. Rajan Chadda? I am Rohit Kapoor. I called you two days ago…"

"Yes, I remember," the old man replied. "You can unlatch the gate to open it; it's not locked."

The young man stepped through the gate, closed and latched it behind him, and walked up the concrete driveway towards the veranda.

"You are punctual," the old man observed.

"I try to be, sir," Rohit replied, smiling. "I have found that people are more receptive to journalists who arrive on time and waste as little of their time as possible."

"A very wise policy," Mr. Chadda said. "Come and sit down." He indicated the chair next to him on the veranda. "I trust you will not mind conducting your interview here, or would you prefer to go indoors?"

"This is fine, sir," Rohit said. "The weather is very pleasant." He slipped his bag off his shoulder and sat down, placing the bag on the polished concrete floor next to him.

"Now, first of all, what would you like to drink?" asked Mr. Chadda. "Chai? Or some cold *nimbu-pani* (lemonade), perhaps?"

"Oh, please don't bother about refreshments, sir."

"It's no bother. Now, what will it be?"

"Nimbu-pani would be fine, sir."

Mr. Chadda heaved himself to his feet. "I'll be back in a few minutes."

He returned bearing two tall glasses filled with lime-green liquid and ice. He handed one of the glasses to the young man and carefully sat down in his chair.

The lemonade was aromatic with the scent of fresh ginger and mint. Rohit took a swallow and said, appreciatively: "Delicious! Thank you, sir."

Mr. Chadda took a swallow from his glass and said, "Now, from what I gathered from your telephone call, you are interviewing people who were actually displaced by the partition of 1947 which split India into two separate countries – India and Pakistan, correct?"

"Yes, sir. The partition was deeply scarring and traumatic for those who were displaced, changing their lives dramatically, uprooting them from places and communities where they had lived for generations. The survivors of the partition are now all quite old, and many have passed away. I wish to capture as many individual stories of those remaining as possible, before they are lost forever. Me and my team of researchers are attempting to document these actual, authentic experiences and make them available on a website and as a book."

"A very laudable effort," Mr. Chadda said. He looked inquiringly at his visitor. "Now, how shall we begin?"

Rohit reached down and unzipped the bag which lay at his feet. He extracted a small portable tape recorder from it and a pad of ruled paper. He set the tape recorder down on the small table that stood between their two chairs.

"I hope you have no objection to being recorded, sir."

"No, none at all. Do you want me to speak directly into the machine?"

"Oh, there is no need to do that, sir," Rohit replied. "It has a very powerful microphone, so you can make yourself comfortable and lean back in your chair, if you wish, and speak in a normal tone of voice."

"Very well. Shall I begin?"

"Just one moment, sir." Rohit switched on the tape recorder and pressed the red 'Rec' button. "You can begin now."

§

(Mr. Chadda's narrative)

I well remember the night of the 14th of August, 1947. The midnight bells pealed and ushered in the dawn of freedom in India, and people rejoiced that roughly two hundred years of British rule had ended.

I was 14 years old at the time and lived with my parents in a large house in Lahore. My father owned a textile business there, and he was prospering. My mother was a housewife, and I was studying at the Sacred Heart School in the city.

I was aware that a new country named Pakistan was in the process of being created that was to be the new home for the Muslims of India. It made my father very upset. I heard him talk about it often, quite bitterly, after the plan was announced in the weeks leading up to the partition. He felt, as did Mahatma Gandhi and some other prominent leaders, that there was no need to split India into two separate countries. My father would often say that the lives of Hindus and Muslims in India were inexorably intertwined, and point out that according to historians, the first Muslims arrived in predominantly Hindu India between the 8th and 11th centuries AD, from what was then known as Persia.

After it was decided that a separate country, Pakistan, would be carved out of a portion of India, the actual borders that had been drawn up dividing India and Pakistan was disseminated to the public on the 17th of August, 1947.

We discovered that the city of Lahore, where we lived and where my father had his business, would now fall within the newly created Pakistan. Even then, my father never imagined that it would be a problem – after all, his Hindu family had lived for many decades in Lahore in peaceful co-existence with their Muslim neighbors, as had many other Hindu families. At the time, a third of Lahore's population were Hindus.

On the morning of the 18th of August, which was the day following the finalization of the borders between the two countries, our day began pretty much as usual. We all breakfasted together, and afterwards, I got ready to go to school, while my father was getting ready to drive to his factory.

Suddenly, there was a loud knocking on our front door. When my father opened it, our next-door neighbor, a Muslim gentleman named Syed Khan, dashed in. Syed and my father were about the same age and good friends. He would come over often to our house in the evenings after dinner, and he and Father would sit on the veranda and talk about anything and everything that came to their minds: politics, the economy, music, books. I called him Syed uncle, and his son Nasir was my classmate and best friend.

I noticed that Syed was not looking at all like his usual calm, cheerful self, but breathing hard and looking extremely distraught. Without any preamble, he cried: "You must leave the city immediately, if you value your life!"

My father stared at him, astonished. "What on earth do you mean, Syed?"

"I heard that vigilante mobs are attacking Hindu households all over the city!" Syed uncle said.

"Are you sure about this, my friend?" asked my father. "I don't understand — why are Hindus being attacked?"

"Because Lahore now falls within Pakistan," Syed replied.

"Why should that matter?" asked my father. "Hindus have lived peacefully in this city for many generations alongside our Muslim friends and neighbors. We all know each other well."

"I don't know why it's happening," our neighbor said, looking very distressed. "All I know is what I've heard from authentic sources — Hindu families are being killed all over the city."

Hearing the commotion, my mother had now come into the hall, where the three of us were standing, and was staring at us with wide, frightened eyes.

My father shook his head in disbelief. He trusted his good friend, but I could tell that he was having a hard time coming to terms with what he was being told. "But, Syed, what about the police? They will surely stop the mob, and keep us safe."

"I heard that the police are overwhelmed," responded Syed. "Also, there is a great deal of confusion among the authorities; no one expected this level of violence to occur. They have been unable to stop the bloodshed."

My father was staring at him uncertainly, wondering if the situation was as bad as his friend claimed it to be. He came to a sudden decision.

"I was on the verge of leaving for my factory just now," he said. "Let me go and take a look and make sure that everything is all right there."

Syed stared at him, aghast. "You shouldn't go, *bhaijan*! You could get yourself killed!"

"Come, come, it can't be as bad as all that," my father said, trying to muster up a smile.

"Based on what I heard, it is, I tell you!"

My father can be a stubborn man. He said, determinedly: "Syed, if what you say is true, that is all the more reason for me to go to my factory and make sure that everything there is all right."

Syed uncle saw that my father's mind was made up. He said, "Well then, at least let me take you in my car. It has Government license plates." Syed was a high-ranking government official. "We will be safer in it — if we encounter a mob, they will think that we are government officials, and leave us alone."

He then eyed the way my father was dressed, in a long-sleeved shirt and slacks, which was his typical outfit when he went to work. "But before we go, please change into something that makes you look Muslim. Take off that shirt and put on a kurta over your slacks. I will bring you a cap that we Muslims habitually wear; I have many extra ones."

"Is all that really necessary, Syed?" demanded my father.

"Please trust me," our neighbor implored earnestly. "I heard that the rioting and violence is really bad. Even if the news I've heard has been exaggerated, it can do no harm to take extra precautions. And please tell your son to stay home. Do not put his life at risk by sending him off to school today."

"Very well," said my father reluctantly.

So I ended up staying at home while Syed uncle and my father set off together in Syed's car. My poor mother was so nervous! She would go to the front windows and peer through them every fifteen minutes or so.

Finally, an hour and a half later, I heard her draw a big sigh of relief. I joined her at the window and saw that Syed uncle's car had just pulled up outside our house.

My father walked in. He was pale and trembling. He sank into a chair in our front hall and covered his face with his hands. "Oh, my God…"

When he raised his head, my mother and I saw that his face was streaked with tears. I was stunned — I had never seen my father cry before.

"It's horrible out there," my father whispered. "My factory is completely wrecked. I saw the body of my foreman, Chimmanlal, and some of my workers literally hacked to pieces, lying there in pools of blood. The streets are littered with corpses — men, women, and even children. There are angry mobs rampaging around, armed with swords, knives, and spears."

He looked directly at my mother. "We have to leave, if we wish to stay alive. The mobs will arrive here sooner or later. Let us pack what we can into suitcases. There's a train leaving for India in two hours. Syed said that he will take us to the train station in his car."

"But what about our house, in which we've lived for so long, our furniture, our belongings —" my mother stammered.

"We have to leave it all!" said my father, fiercely. "There's no time to worry about such things! It's a matter of life and death."

He stood shakily to his feet, and his voice grew more gentle. "I am very sorry, my dear, but we have no choice. Now please go and start packing. Wear a *salwar-kameez* and a scarf over your head so that you look like a Muslim lady. Rajan, take off your school uniform and put on a kurta."

Feeling terrified, I rushed off to my bedroom, where I changed into a kurta and slacks, and packed a suitcase with as many of my clothes as I could. I left behind my cricket bat, my books, and other items I treasured — my father said that we neither had the time nor space for those things.

We piled into Syed's car after putting our suitcases in the trunk, and began an anxiety filled ride to the train station. As long as I live, I will never forget the horrifying sights that met my eyes along the way. Like my father had said, the streets were literally strewn with corpses — men, women, even little children. My mother tried to cover my eyes with her hand, but I pushed her hand aside. She kept praying "*Harey Ram, harey Ram*" under her breath. We could see pillars of smoke rising all over the city, and hear hoarse cries and screams coming from a distance.

There was one terrifying moment when a small group of militants armed with wicked looking swords and knives halted the car. Their leader approached Syed and demanded to know where we were going.

"I am a Government Official," Syed said, haughtily. What courage it must have taken him not to exhibit the fear he surely must have felt inside! "Didn't you see the Government License Plates on the car?" He pulled out his Government-issued ID and thrust it at the militant's face. "Now, are you going to let me and my family proceed?"

The militant leader's fierce, bloodshot eyes looked us over. Seeing us all dressed in outfits as worn by a typical Muslim family, in conjunction with Syed's confident manner, must have convinced him of our bona fides, for he stepped back and waved us on.

We drew a collective breath of relief. "Thank God you suggested that we dress up as Muslims, Syed," my father whispered.

We were fortunate to reach the train station without further incident.

There was a mass of people streaming into the station. We were surprised, but grateful, to see that the station was guarded by soldiers. "I'm glad that our government has at least done this much," Syed remarked, grimly.

We took our suitcases out of the trunk and my father and Syed embraced each other. Tears sprang into their eyes. "I'll never forget what you have done for me today, my friend," my father said, in a voice choked with emotion.

"I hope we are able to see each other again someday," Syed said. "*Khuda hafiz* (May God be with you)."

After Syed got back into his car and drove away, my father muttered, with a great deal of sadness, "I hope he doesn't get into trouble for helping us."

The train was already packed to the brim with people, but we managed to squeeze into a compartment. Many of those on the train were wounded and bleeding. Everyone looked dazed and terrified.

After what felt like an eternity, the train got underway. It gathered speed as it sped through the town and soon we were travelling through the open countryside. By the side of the tracks, we saw huge columns of people trudging towards the Indian border, carrying whatever they possessed on their backs and in bullock carts. These were villagers fleeing the homes they had lived in peacefully for decades. I heard later that some of these columns of refugees were attacked by militants and massacred.

The people on the train began to breathe a little easier as the train chugged on. But our troubles were far from over.

There's a small station, Wagah, that was the last scheduled stop for the train on what was now the Pakistani side of the newly formed border with India. The train began to slow down as it approached Wagah station. We saw, to our horror, that the platform was full of armed militants brandishing swords, knives, spears, and other weapons. We could not make out what they were yelling over the noise and clamor of the train, but it seemed apparent that they intended to board the train and kill us.

The women in our compartment began to scream and cry, while the children clung to them, terrified. Many of the older women clasped their hands, closed their eyes, and began to pray loudly, chanting *"Baghwan, hamey bachao* (God save us)" over and over again. Some of the men ran up and down the length of the train, locking the compartment doors and yelling at the passengers to step back from open windows.

Then, like a miracle, as if in response to our prayers, the train started speeding up again.

By the time it arrived at the Wagah station platform, it was going quite fast. One could tell that the militants amassed on the platform were taken aback; they had expected the train to slow down and stop. A few of the bolder ones tried to jump on, but were thrown off by the shaking and swaying of the train as it sped through the station. We heard later that there was a British officer stationed in the train's engine compartment, and he ordered the engine driver to speed up instead of stopping. That is what saved our lives.

We also heard that the next train behind us was not so fortunate, and it arrived on the Indian side of the border full of bloody corpses.

After that scare at Wagah Station, the train proceeded without any further incident till we arrived at Amritsar, in India, exhausted but very thankful to be alive.

§

Mr. Rajan Chadda paused and took a big swallow of lemonade from his glass. His eyes were gazing unseeingly at his green lawn, and his face was masked by a look of utter sadness. He took a deep breath, shook his head, and said:

"To this day, I have never really understood all the bloodshed and madness that took place after partition was announced. Who carried out these killings? It certainly wasn't people like my friend and neighbor Syed, a Muslim who risked his own life to save us, a Hindu family. Similarly, I have heard of many Hindus in India who saved the lives of their Muslim neighbors and friends by either hiding them in their house or helping them flee to safety."

"You know, sir, it's interesting that you should wonder as to who was responsible for the bloodshed," said the young journalist, Rohit. "During my interviews with survivors of that terrible time, almost everyone said just that — who were the anarchists carrying out these massacres? They were certainly not our neighbors and friends. I talked recently to an old Hindu lady who had lived with her family in a small village that fell on the Pakistan side of the border after the new borders were drawn up. She said, 'I didn't recognize any of the assassins who came to our village to kill. I can tell you this much: they were certainly not our Muslim neighbors in the village. We all knew each other. The killers came from somewhere else.' Just like in your case, her Muslim neighbors helped her family escape."

"Yes, I still find it hard to believe official accounts that friends and neighbors who had lived side by side peacefully for decades suddenly turned on each other," Rajan Chadda said.

"Which leads to another key question, who started the riots and violence?" Rohit said.

"My view is that a few immoral politicians ignited the violence," Mr. Chadda replied. "That has happened throughout history, in many parts of the world. Look at what happened in Germany — it took just one fanatical leader, Hitler, to set in motion one of the biggest mass murders of an ethnic group that the world has ever witnessed."

"That's very true, sir," Rohit said, thoughtfully.

"Another problem was that the leaders of both India and the newly formed Pakistan never anticipated that partition would bring about the level of violence that took place, and were totally unprepared for it," Mr. Chadda went on. "Also, the British, in preparation for the transfer of power, had already withdrawn most of their troops by that time, so they didn't have the manpower to quell the riots. The police forces were also unprepared and did not receive proper orders; there was a great deal of bureaucratic confusion at the time. So a few fanatical mobs were able to roam unchecked and create havoc. At least, that's what I think."

"Your thinking falls in line with that of many of the other survivors I've talked to," Rohit said. "Now, sir, before I conclude the interview, I would like to ask whether there's anything else you would like to add."

Mr. Chadda smiled wryly. "Just this: unfortunately, the horrific violence that accompanied partition created a deep distrust between India and Pakistan that exists to this day. It's sad, because for thousands of years we were just one nation."

"Well, sir, in all fairness, events like the terrorist attack on Mumbai in November 2008 by ten members of an extremist Islamic terrorist organization based in Pakistan, in which 164 people were killed, doesn't help to raise the level of trust between the two countries."

Mr. Chadda heaved a deep sigh. "No, it doesn't. We can only hope that the world heeds the words of Mahatma Gandhi: 'An eye for an eye makes the whole world blind'. He tried so hard to convince India and the world that change can, and should, be brought about through peaceful, non-violent means. But despite his messages of peace, the poor man was himself violently assassinated, with three bullets pumped into his frail body by an extremist. And even now, secular riots take place from time to time. Perhaps human beings will never learn from the lessons of history. Perhaps they don't want to."

After the young journalist had packed up his equipment and left, Mr. Chadda continued to sit on the veranda for a little while, gazing at his front garden, his mind far away.

The day was beginning to get warm. He got to his feet, a little stiff from having sat for so long, picked up the two empty glasses, and walked into the cool interior of his house. Just as he returned to the living room after depositing the empty glasses in the kitchen sink, the telephone, which stood on a tall table by the side of his armchair, rang shrilly. He went over, picked up the receiver, and said, "Hello?" As the voice on the other end responded, a broad smile lit up his face.

"Nasir! So good to hear from you! How are you? How's the family? All good? Great! You know, it's really a coincidence that you should call me today of all days, because I was just talking about your father and how he helped us get to safety back in 1947…"

The Sacred Grove

The little Morris Minor sedan drove steadily along the highway in deep southern India. The year was 1952, some five years after India's independence from British rule. The driver, a lean middle aged man with graying hair, was sitting back in his seat, relaxed, enjoying the sight of the well paved road stretching out ahead of him. The slim, pretty lady seated in the passenger seat next to him was glancing out of the window at the surrounding green countryside.

Suddenly, the lady remarked: "You built this road, didn't you, husband?"

The man smiled. "I was on the crew that constructed it, yes."

They were coming up to a village on the right hand side of the highway. The driver eased the pressure of his foot on the accelerator, and the car began to slow down. Up ahead, the highway ran straight towards a grove of tamarind trees surrounding what appeared to be a small, very old shrine with crumbling walls of heavy gray stone. As they drove nearer, the lady noticed that the road came to within ten yards of the tamarind grove, then veered off to the left to form a rough semicircle that went around it, before resuming its straight-line progress on the other side.

"How nice!" exclaimed the lady. "You built the road

to go around the shrine rather than going straight through."

"Not by choice," her husband remarked.

His wife turned her head to look at him. There was a far-away look in her husband's eyes, as though he was recalling something from years ago.

"What do you mean?" she asked.

"We were forced to build the road to go around the grove, although it would have been far cheaper to build it to go straight on through."

"Who forced you? Religious agitators?"

"No, actually by what appeared to be a supernatural spirit," her husband replied.

The lady opened her eyes wide at this. "A supernatural spirit?" she echoed. "You're joking, aren't you?"

"No, I'm being absolutely serious," her husband said. "There are truly no other words to describe what happened. But perhaps I had better tell you the whole story…"

§

It was around 1931 when we began construction of this road. As you know, the British ruled over most of India at the time. They had realized the importance of a good transportation system to facilitate the movement of goods and army vehicles to strengthen their hold over the country, and hence had been constructing a network of railway lines and highways like this one all over India.

I was the Junior Engineer on the project to build this particular highway. The Engineer in Charge was a tall, powerfully built Englishman named John Baker. He was a tough man whose primary focus was the job on hand and who gave little thought to the feelings of the local Indians he encountered. The British Administrators liked him because whatever his faults, he got things done in a timely manner and within budget. The construction crew consisted of Indian laborers. A few British soldiers were also along, to ensure our safety.

Our daily work routine was that we would build as much of the road as we could during the day, then set up tents along the roadside to sleep in at night. The crew included two Indian cooks who prepared our daily meals. The provisions, stoves, tents, and other camping gear were all carried along in a couple of large trucks.

There had been the usual snags from time to time, unavoidable in any major construction project, but on the whole work on the road had pretty much gone according to plan. Then one day we arrived at this grove of old tamarind trees, in the center of which stood the small shrine, directly in the path of the proposed roadway. Even back in those days, the shrine was almost in ruins and had an abandoned air.

For the road to continue in a straight line, it would have to cut through the tamarind grove and the small shrine would have to be demolished. Since the shrine was old and falling into ruin, we didn't anticipate any problems. There was a village nearby, but it stood to one side and didn't fall in the path of the proposed highway.

We had completed construction of the roadway up to a point some fifteen yards in front of the tamarind grove by lunchtime. Baker decided to halt work for lunch. So we sat by the roadside, in the shade of some nearby trees, and began to eat. As was customary, Baker and I sat on camp chairs next to each other. I will say this for Baker: he always treated me pretty well, and generally followed my suggestions, although he never let anyone forget that he was the ultimate boss.

We had just finished our lunch when we noticed a group of men approaching us from the nearby village, spearheaded by a priest. They were jabbering away in the Tamil dialect common in that district, and appeared to be in a state of considerable agitation, especially the priest.

Baker turned to me with a quizzical look, and asked: "What do they want, Krishna?" I knew both English and Tamil well, and one of my roles was to act as Baker's interpreter when communicating with the farmers and other country people we encountered during the course of our construction project.

By then, the villagers and priest had arrived at where Baker and I were seated. I got up from my camp chair and addressed the priest, bringing the palms of my hands together in a respectful greeting, and asked in Tamil: "What is the matter, *shastrigal*?"

"My son," the priest said, "Are you planning to build the road through that grove of tamarind trees?"

"That is our plan, yes," I replied.

"You must not!" the priest exclaimed. "That grove is sacred. You see that shrine in the middle? Our ancient legends say that Ravana himself rested in that shrine for one night and meditated. It is said that whoever disturbs that shrine, or any of the trees, will come to considerable harm."

I was taken aback, and many of our crew of laborers,

who had gathered nearby, began murmuring fearfully among themselves. Baker, meanwhile, was bristling with curiosity, and demanded to be told what was being said.

After I translated, Baker snorted. "Stuff and nonsense!" he barked. "Who is this Ravana?"

How best to describe him? I knew that Baker would not have the patience to listen to a long explanation. After thinking for a few moments, I said: "In our ancient texts, Ravana is portrayed as a demon king with tremendous powers."

Baker snorted with derision. "Is he, now? Well, tell the priest that I fear no demon!"

I dutifully translated this to the priest, whose eyes grew wide with terror.

"The Englishman must not say that!" he cried. "If he defies the spirit of Ravana, he will surely be punished."

After I conveyed this message to Baker, he grew very red in the face and shouted: "I fear no Ravana! And to prove it, I am going to pull down the first tree in that grove myself!"

There was a massive tamarind tree that stood directly in the path of the roadway, on the edge of the grove. Ignoring the priest's almost tearful entreaties, the big Englishman ordered some of the scared workers to fasten a chain around the tree. The other end of the chain was fastened to one of the powerful bulldozers. Baker climbed into the driver's seat, started up the engine, and shifted the gear into reverse.

The bulldozer began to back up and the chain that had been fastened around the tree trunk became taut. Baker grimly opened up the throttle further and the bulldozer took up the strain, inching slowly backwards.

The priest's face was contorted with fear, and he was chanting prayers loudly in Sanskrit.

Suddenly there was a loud *crack!* sound and the metal chain snapped. The broken end of the chain came flying through the air towards the bulldozer. Baker ducked just in time, and it went whirling past his head. A mere second later, a scream of agony rent the air.

We were paralyzed for a few moments, then rushed forward. The broken end of the chain had flown past Baker, who had ducked, and smashed into the skull of one of the laborers standing nearby. A quick examination proved that he was dead, his head battered beyond recognition.

The priest turned to me. "See!" he cried. "The wrath of Ravana will not be denied! Did I not warn the Englishman? Now you have needlessly lost a life. I beg you to alter the course of the road, and leave Ravana's spirit in peace."

After I had translated this for Baker's benefit, it only served to anger him further.

"All of you listen to me!" he bellowed. "What happened was just an accident! The chain probably had a weak link to begin with. My job is to build this road in the most efficient way possible, and that means cutting straight through that blasted grove! And I am going to do it, even if I have to pull up every tree that stands in our way and demolish the shrine myself!"

Our crew was thoroughly terrified by this time, and no amount of yelling and cursing from Baker could get them to go near the tamarind grove. So Baker himself took another set of chains, and with two of the British soldiers helping him, fastened them around the tree and attached the other end to the bulldozer, as before. He climbed into the driver's seat once again and began backing up the powerful machine.

An electric, fearful atmosphere hung over the spot as we all watched breathlessly. The priest had resumed chanting prayers, and many of the laborers were joining in.

Baker opened the throttle wide, the bulldozer's engine roared, but the tree would not budge. To those of us watching, it seemed like the tree was resisting the pull of the powerful bulldozer with some uncanny strength.

But finally, with a loud groan, as though of despair, the tree began to be pulled up out of the earth. A few minutes later, the entire tree toppled over to one side, exposing its roots.

Shrieks of terror arose from among the laborers.

For there entwined firmly among the roots was a human skeleton!

Even I was thoroughly shaken, I must admit. But not Baker. He jumped down from the bulldozer, and striding forward, surveyed the skeleton. Turning to the priest, he shouted: "Look, here is your demon! Vanquished!"

The priest shook his head, fearfully. Turning to me, he implored: "The Englishman just does not understand! Those bones are not Ravana — he was ten, twenty times as large! That skeleton must have been some foolish man who dared to defile the grove and perished as a result."

I translated this to Baker, who just laughed. Having managed to uproot one tree, he was no doubt feeling triumphant. "Krishna, tell the men that I am going to take those bones and bury them off to one side. Tell them also that after that, I guarantee that we will not have any more problems with this grove!"

The bones were buried in a spot some distance away, with Baker and the British soldiers handling the whole grisly task themselves, since none of the Indian laborers could be persuaded to help, despite threats and curses.

By the time Baker was done, the sun was beginning to sink low on the horizon. He decided to postpone work on the road until the next morning. I think he must have felt that a good night's sleep would fortify the crew's spirits and have them be more prepared to tackle the tamarind grove and the shrine the next day. The priest and villagers had left by that time.

Baker invited me to have dinner with him in his tent. Being the Engineer in charge, he had a large tent all to himself. I picked up my plate of vegetarian food from the cook, and made my way there. When I arrived, I found Baker seated in front of a small table set up in the middle of his tent, his plate of food and a glass containing a generous measure of whiskey in front of him. He did not offer me any, for he knew that I did not drink. After I had seated myself, he raised his glass, said "Cheers," and polished off half of the whiskey in one gulp. He started gobbling up his dinner ravenously — all the hard work this afternoon must have given him a keen appetite. After he was finished, he leaned back in his camp chair, fixed his sharp blue eyes upon me and asked:

"Well, what do you make of it, Krishna? You were born and raised in this land. Do you believe in all this demon nonsense?"

I replied cautiously, "Sir, we Indians on the whole are a very religious people, and most of us believe in our ancient legends. We have all heard about Ravana from a young age."

Then I was struck by an inspiration, and said: "Sir, don't some of the ancient legends in England and Europe talk about witches and demons and other evil spirits? And even the Bible talks about Satan, does it not?"

Baker stared at me, as if this had never occurred to him. And in truth, it probably hadn't. He finally said slowly, "You're right."

Baker's acceptance of my argument made me feel like I had scored a minor victory. Quickly, so as to not lose my advantage, I continued: "In all fairness, sir, superstitions and fables about demons and evil spirits are not unique to India, but exist all over the world — even in England. So you can't really blame the village priest for believing in Ravana and trying to warn us, and our laborers for believing him. When the chain broke and killed one of their own, it only served to solidify their belief in the legend." I paused and added, "To be quite honest, I too began to wonder whether that grove was somehow protected by some unseen spirit."

Baker jumped to his feet and began pacing up and down his tent. He stopped, wiped his hand across his brow, and said: "Look, Krishna, I am not the type who can readily enter into a theological discussion about demons and angels and superstitions. I am an engineer, a practical man who deals with facts. Granted, the chain snapped, but I still firmly believe that it broke because it was old, and not because of some evil spirit. Now, regarding the skeleton we unearthed. To me, all that it appears to indicate is that someone got buried in that spot a long time ago. Perhaps someone was murdered and the body buried there. Then the murderer, or murderers, spread the story of an evil spirit, and over the years the story grew and grew to become one of Ravana. Now, isn't that possible?"

I fell silent. Baker in turn had given me food for thought. What he said made sense. But on the other hand...

Baker paused in his perambulations, faced me, and went on: "My superiors expect me to construct this highway in the most efficient manner possible, while taking into account practicality, safety, and cost. How would it look if I were to tell them: 'I had to curve the road around a grove of trees because I was told it is possessed by a demon'? I would become a laughing stock."

"I understand, sir," I said.

Baker smiled with relief. "Good man! Well, let's not worry about it any more. We will proceed tomorrow and see what happens. Now go and get a good night's sleep."

But nothing could have prepared us for the shock that awaited us the following morning.

On the fringe of the tamarind grove, directly in the proposed path of the roadway, the ground was split by a deep fissure a couple of feet in width and stretching over ten yards in length!

Typical of him, Baker's initial reaction was that the fissure was man-made. He grew furious and was prepared to yell and threaten our crew of Indian laborers until he discovered who amongst them had done this. He was also getting ready to order the British soldiers to round up every able-bodied man in the nearby village and bring them to him for questioning.

I finally managed to calm Baker down to the point where he would listen to me. I pointed out to him that for any one person, or a group of men, to dig such a deep, long, and wide fissure literally overnight, without making enough sound to wake us, was impossible. I took Baker to the edge of the fissure and showed him how deep it was. Standing at the edge, one couldn't even see the bottom. The fissure looked like the earth had cracked open at that point, the way it happens sometimes in the aftermath of an earthquake. The problem was, none of us had felt the slightest tremor during the night.

At that point, Baker gave up. He must have realized that he had run up against something that even his engineering mind couldn't explain or conquer.

So we altered our plans and proceeded to build the road in a wide loop around the tamarind grove, the way you see it now.

§

Krishna stopped his narrative and glanced sideways at his wife. She had been listening with rapt attention, without interrupting him. She had always been a good listener.

"Well, what do you think?" he asked.

She shook her head in amazement. "What an incredible story! It just goes to show, there are things that happen in this world that we just do not understand."

"There are more things in heaven and Earth, Horatio, than are dreamt of in your philosophy," Krishna said. He paused and added, with a mischievous glint in his eyes, "That's a quotation from Shakespeare, by the way."

"Of course I know it's from Shakespeare!" his wife retorted.

Krishna chuckled. "I was only teasing you. I know that you would recognize the quotation — you have a degree in Literature, after all."

"Always teasing!" his wife said. Then she calmed down, stretched out her hand and squeezed his arm, fondly. "While I am sorry to hear that one of the laborers got killed while Baker was defying the grove, I am so glad that nothing happened to you."

Author's Notes & Acknowledgements

If you enjoyed reading this book, kindly post your review on Amazon, Facebook, Goodreads, and other social media. That really helps relatively unknown authors like myself to get better known.

Also, kindly tell your friends and relatives about this book. All of my books are available on Amazon, both as paperback and as a Kindle edition.

The past four years (at the time this is written) since my beloved wife passed away have not been easy. I think of my beloved every day, and miss her comforting presence. The year 2020, in particular, was extremely hard (as it was for most of us) as the Covid-19 pandemic kept me confined to my home for the most part. Thank God for modern forms of communication (Cellphone, WhatsApp, Zoom, etc.) that enabled me to keep in regular touch with others.

I would like to give special thanks to the following people for providing me their love and support, which enabled me to carry on under very difficult circumstances:

My wonderful daughter Amrita, who has been a rock; my beloved mother Rugminy; my sister Revathy & her husband Kris; my wife's two sisters Gomathy & Venil; my nephews Anish & Arjun and their wives; my son Ashwin; numerous cousins on both sides of the family; my aunts; my wife's aunts & uncles; and several good friends here in Las Vegas and around the country. Special thanks to my old classmates from my schooldays in India, who kept in touch with me via daily texts and periodic phone calls.

I would be remiss not to give special thanks to journalist Swetha Amit. I am truly grateful to her for reviewing my book *"Radha's Revenge & Other Stories"* and for taking the time and effort to interview me. Swetha is an avid reader who has read more books than anyone can count (she read over 100 books in 2020 alone!), so her positive review of my book means a great deal.

Likewise, special thanks to author Carrie Ann Lahain, whose enthusiastic reviews of my books have left me feeling humbled and grateful.

And last but not least, my grateful thanks to my dear cousin Hari Padmanabhan for providing immense help by proofing my manuscript and catching quite a few typos that had eluded my eyes. Paddu (as he's known in our family) and I have shared many rambunctious adventures in our younger days (the details of which shall remain a closely guarded secret!). After my beloved Vidya passed away, he has made a special effort to cheer me up whenever I feel depressed.

Reviews for the author's earlier publications

Radha's Revenge & Other Stories

"*I read Radha's Revenge & Other Stories right after I'd moved across the country. How wonderful to fall into this author's beautifully written world after a stressful day unpacking or arranging utility service or trying to figure out which electrical outlet is the one served by the bedroom light switch. Each story is its own self-contained universe. Yet, taken together, they showcase Gopal Ramanan's particular gift for balancing realism with imagination and just the right amount of humor.*"
Carrie Ann Lahain, Author of *Morgrim's Wood, The Ways of Mud and Bone*, and other novels.

"*In Radha's Revenge & Other Stories, Gopal Ramanan masterfully brings his characters, settings, and plots to life. I felt the broken heart, the joy, the grief, the regret, and the triumph as the characters moved through the sometimes surprising plot lines. My favorites are those in which the best qualities of human character are juxtaposed against the worst and the best wins, though I also enjoyed those stories that took a little poke at our human foibles, machinations, and materialism of the modern world....A wonderful collection.*"
Kimberlee J Benart, ReadersFavorite.com

"*From children running away from alcoholic uncles towards a hopeful future, dealing with sexual harassment at work places, spiritual encounters, acts of kindness to some interesting twists - the author weaves some poignant tales in his simple yet lucid style of writing. The narrative style took me back to some of the works written by the great Indian writer R.K. Narayan. The characters and instances captured in these stories are relatable and memorable. A couple of stories that tugged the strings of*

my heart were 'An Act of Kindness' and 'The Shoeshine Boy'. Some of these tales leave you moist eyed while others mirror reality. This is one collection of stirring tales that you wouldn't want to miss."
Swetha Amith, Journalist.

"This is definitely a must read. Written in a simple straightforward manner, the stories were so interesting that I could not put the book down and finished the book at one sitting. I'm eagerly waiting for his next book."
Meenakshi Narayanan

"Ideal rainy day read - with a cup of hot tea, and this lovely book, I've been in bliss this afternoon. The heart-warming short stories set in India are full of understanding and kindness towards the world. I don't want to give away spoilers, but the titular narrative is not the blood and gore the word "revenge" normally conjures up. I heartily recommend this book to anyone who wants to feel uplifted in today's world. Each story has its own twists and turns, and I was drawn into each tale."

R.D.

"I read this collection of short stories in one sitting. There is a story in the collection for everyone - the romantic, the comedy lover, the thrill seeker . This book is the author's 3rd book and I have read them all. His writing style is reminiscent of 2 of my favorite Indian authors - Ruskin Bond and R.K. Narayan. The author uses simple language so the focus stays on the stories."

Komala Krishnaswamy

Murder of a Judge

"Author Gopal Ramanan gives us well-defined characters and a crisply paced plot full of unexpected twists. He does a wonderful job evoking the sights and sounds of his setting, a small city in southern India. I enjoyed this window on the everyday lives of a people and place so far removed from my own world here in America."

"MURDER OF A JUDGE is a quick, satisfying reading experience, and Inspector Anand is the kind of smart, honorable sleuth you want to read about again and again."

"The author has struck a perfect balance between an easy pace that allows the reader to savor every moment and a suspenseful unfolding of the plot worthy of the genre. I thoroughly enjoyed both the aspects."

"It was very suspenseful and kept me guessing who did it until the very end."

"Hope we continue to enjoy Inspector Anand's mystery solving skills in upcoming novels!"

Made in the USA
Middletown, DE
20 September 2021